The Abandonment of Earth

.

H.R MacDonald

H.R MacDonald

Disclaimer and Copyright

To the People of Sussex

Past, Present and Future.

"We Wunt Be Druv!"

Prologue

The crackle of gunfire in the distance added to the early morning birdsong of the cold English morning. The mist blowing down from the Downs in waves and filling the low-lying plateau which was covered in unploughed empty fields and heavy, dark woodland. Empty roads and empty villages which were once bustling with people and vehicles. Now still, and stagnant. The cloudy sky allowing a speck of sunlight to break through and illuminate the countryside and the few people still struggling within it.

A group of men wandered along the old main road towards the ancient city of Chichester with its half-destroyed cathedral looming in the distance miles away. They were all heavily armed with mêlée weapons, shields and tattered homemade armour, made from scrap metal and old chicken wire. Their appearance was that of despair. Unwashed and unpruned adding to the tattered nature of their dress. Eyes sunken from many sleepless nights in the cold Sussex wilderness.

Their way was blocked by a barrier of burnt out car chassis which had been dragged across the tarmac which was now covered in a fine layer of weeds which had sprung up after the first few weeks of the collapse. They stopped. Anxious and agitated by the constant, distant sound of gunfire which had been following them ever since they started their journey before dawn from the small village of Singleton, deep within the walls of the Downs.

They muttered to themselves, wondering what to do next. Asking questions such as "Was this roadblock put their on purpose?", "Are we being watched?", "Is there anyone left here?". They agreed that one of them should go ahead and see if the way is clear, while the rest waited on the outskirts of the village they had just arrived at, getting out their portable stove for a quick and bland breakfast of oats and water.

The unlucky soul who was chosen to go ahead climbed over the barricade covering himself in ash and soot, giving rise to the horrible smell of burnt plastic, rubber and the ever-present smell of smoke which was now the most common of smells after rotting flesh.

The village was in ruins. Buildings like empty bodies with their masonry and brickwork shattered, the occasional piece of clothing flittered in the wind like some kind of primordial wind sock. It was the most depressing of sights. He wandered along the main street looking for any sign of life, any stirring of human activity past or present which could tell him if there were inhabitants in this long-forgotten village.

He came to the site of what was the only shop in the village, its signage still bright in the morning light but broken in half and hanging precariously close to the limits of the grimy brick faced building. Stepping over broken glass through the once large main window which was now a gloomy portal into the darkness of the shop floor behind. The crunch sounded like it could have been heard leagues away due to the complete and utter silence that had now descended.

The shop was airy and rather large for such a small settlement and its walls were long since picked clean of anything valuable or edible. All that was left were the wrappers and cartoons from food products, the gleam of steel from empty shelves and the ever-present smell of stale and rotting produce. He looked in a few crevices around the empty shelves and behind the counter. Thinking to himself "maybe someone has left some food hidden or something valuable". Behind the counter there was even more darkness, and in his haste, he didn't see the rolled sleeping bag. Tripping, he fell and almost knocked himself senseless on the marble counter which had once been the main till. A sleeping bag meant past human habitation which both added excitement but also anxiety.

He found nothing behind the counter and nothing in the main shop floor so he decided to look in the warehouse for anything of value. The door separating him from the warehouse was open a fraction but stuck on something, he struggled, using his shoulder to try and beat the door down to no avail. He then kicked the door just under the handle, a few hard kicks and the door was soon open. Once again darkness filled his view. This time a darkness so full it almost seemed to absorb light.

He tiptoed through the door frame trying to peer into the room, eyes squinting it was impossible to see anything in such low light. He carried a lighter which although a poor source of light would be better than nothing in the complete darkness.

The lighter clicked and the flame sparked to life. What he saw turned his stomach. Piles of bones were dotted around the small warehouse, creating cairn like structures in each corner of the room. Skulls and tibia bones littered the floor having fallen from the cairns creating a terrifying layer obscuring the concrete floor underneath.

The man was used to seeing corpses as it was a common sight in the post-society world but this was too much for him. He vomited violently at this sight. Allowing his lighter to go out and plunging the room back into complete darkness.

He turned to run, his mind in a daze, terror clutching at his soul. Running through the shop he tripped over debris left on the floor and fell head first onto the cold concrete tiles which were littered with fragments of shimmering glass. He was cut and bloody, a shard of glass had cut deeply into his face and wrist, it began to bleed profusely he got back up and continued his escape, albeit at a slower pace now due to his injuries. The running increasing his heart rate and causing the crimson blood to flow quicker from his wounds, leaving a trail of the viscous fluid behind him.

He wanted to scream but couldn't, dizziness and nausea pervading him as he emerged back into the sunlight of the early morning. Crows gathered overhead watching. Knowing that a meal was fast approaching them if only they wait a small time. The blood trail an indicator to them of a great feast.

The man needn't go far as the village was small. He knew he would be safe when he got to his comrades waiting outside the village limits. Safety in numbers was a new motto for the anarchic society that now existed.

The carcass of the burnt-out car was now in his sight and lifted his spirits. He manged to make a faint shout with the small amount of oxygen that was able to escape his lungs.

"Help.... Help".

There was no answer. He stopped running, exhausted and dizzy from blood loss, he got to the wrecked car and lent against it to keep himself balanced. His comrades were nowhere to be seen, their half-prepared meal still sitting on the stove which had gone out. Their weapons lying on the ground in no particular order.

It was at this time that he heard a noise behind him. The sound of foliage moving and then the familiar noise of boots on tarmac. He was startled. Turning as quickly as possible to face the noise.

What faced him caused a second bout of absolute terror. A large figure stood around 20 feet away, wearing all black clothing of the military kind, combat boots which were also jet black in colouring and on his face covered by a worn and frayed balaclava which was also black in colour. What scared the man more was what this figure was holding in his right hand. It was a longsword. Catching the light of the sun it shone but was dripping with blood. The figure just stood in the middle of road silently, his eyes staring at the man who was stuck to the spot in complete shock.

"Who are you?... Where are my friends?" squeaked the man. He knew deep down that he couldn't reason with this figure. But it was the only chance he had left. He couldn't fight because of his injuries and he certainly knew he couldn't escape by running.

The vertigo he was now experiencing became too much and he collapsed to the ground, sitting with his back to the wreck of the car. His life essence was beginning to drain as he began to lose consciousness.

The figure began to walk slowly towards him, the sword held elegantly at his side, not being allowed to touch or drag along the ground but instead staying a few centimetres above it.

From his blurry vision the man could see more movement in the foliage behind the figure, yet more black clad individuals appeared out of the brush and nonchalantly walked onto the tarmac. A dozen figures now crowded onto the road, some holding mêlée weapons and some even brandishing more rare and exotic firearms.

It wasn't long before the figure reached the dying man, standing over him and blocking out the quickly rising sun. The point of the sword being close to the man's face. The figure just stood watching the man, not saying a word. His blue eyes seemed to go straight through the man, but he was looking at his wounds, quietly observing. Before turning around and walking towards the group of individuals who were now making their way up the road towards Chichester.

11

The dying man gasped hoarsely for breath. He knew his end was coming, soaked in his own warm blood, he waited.

The crows began moving closer. Carefully and quietly making their way towards the burnt-out wreck. Sitting in the trees and on the roofs of the outlying buildings of the village. All that could be heard now was the sweet trickle of the flowing river Lavant and the deep, painful breathes of the dying man.

Chapter I

Sunlight crept through the blinds and filtered onto the wall behind with a slight illumination of the small box like room. One wall was covered with open brickwork while the rest were a warm plastered white and were covered in the usual decorations such as a clock, a painting of a hilled landscape and some old framed photos of assorted family pets. The ticking of the clock was slightly subdued by the slight snoring of the young Cyril Quinn who inhabited the aged house.

His bed covered the vast majority of the small but cosy room and was flanked on either side by bedside tables which held his alarm clock and lamp. The alarm clock began to rattle with its droning buzz at 6 o'clock signalling the beginning of another work day for the young man who struggled out of the bed with a yawn and stretch. The humidity and uncomfortable stickiness of the air suggested that the day was going to be one of unbearable heat, common of the past few summers which had graced the Downs. The summer was coming to an end however and it was nature's last parting gift before the autumn rains swept across the land.

After finishing the usual morning routines of

having a wash, getting dressed, combing his
hair, opening his curtains and making his bed,
he then headed down the creaking stairs for the
morning brew of strong English tea of the
breakfast kind. A few letters addressed to him
poked through the letterbox. The officialness of
said letters brought forward a slight uneasiness
in Cyril who had always had anxiety when
dealing with 'officialdom' as he called it. He
would put off opening them until he got home
from work, he thought to himself, he would be
less stressed then.
Before long he was outside locking his door and
getting into the old, beaten up Ford he owned.
Although it was over a decade old it still did its
job and Cyril believed in the philosophy of
'make do and mend' too much jeering and jokes
of his peers and colleagues.
The heat from the blazing sun already made the
inside of the car feel like an oven but with a few
miles behind him it started too cool quickly.
He drove along the narrow roads of the Downs,
to the left of the road one of the many shallow
valleys with the bed of the river Lavant, dried
up during the warm months of summer. It
wouldn't be long before the water from the
chalky Downs would flow from Singleton and
once again fill it with bubbling life. A huge flock
of Sheep were grazing in the green fields and
trying to find shade from the morning sun.

White dots flecking the surrounding fields.
Coming over the next hill he could see the spire
of Chichester cathedral looming in the distance.
That ancient city where Cyril worked had been
the capital of Sussex since time immemorial and
still carried a sort of charm only a rural folk
from that fair county could understand. An
energy which still carried the great changes it
had undergone since the time of the Romans
and Saxons. Some would call it a sinister aura.

The ruralness of the Sussex countryside gave
way to city suburbs and then within minutes the
small built up centre of Chichester. The
cathedral all-consuming within the cluttered
skyline and with the smaller bell tower next to
it. He pulled down a small side street into a
carpark which had seen better days. All kinds of
common weeds and hardy plants growing
through cracks in the tarmac and concrete, a
small buddleia in full bloom with its bright
purple flowers hugged a wall which had the
only patch of sunlight, bees swarming it.
He got to work in a quick time for once. The
streets which streamed into the city from the
four points of the compass were, most of the
time, clogged with traffic of all kinds.

The brutalist office block in which he worked
awaited in front of him. The concrete stained

with rust from various outer mountings, covered in CCTV and long in need of renovation or demolition. Soot and grime clinging to the flaking paint and littered with disgusting looking feral pigeons who were sunbathing. In contrast to the magnificent buildings surrounding it, the office block was like a puss filled sore blighting the area.

Getting out of his car he was filled with a feeling of sadness, he always felt this knowing he was wasting a beautiful day stuck inside a stuffy concrete coffin, toiling away at a dusty desk.

The automatic door lurched open as Cyril marched towards it, letting out a gust of cool conditioned but dry air. The interior of the building was just as dull and depressing as the exterior. Concrete facades and peeling paint and wallpaper being the only difference. Worn and dirty 1970s style carpet bedecked the floor and were illuminated by flickering lights hanging loosely from the ceiling. But the most depressing of all sights was that of the half dead potted plants which were dotted around the lobby in desperate need of some water and real sunlight.

After five years he still felt like a stranger in the decrepit place.

*

"Cyril, your averages are still too low, you will have to stay on an extra hour next week to make up for it, that's all."
Cyril shrugged; it wasn't the first time he had been the focus of his managers team meetings which were held every other day in the small office staffroom. His manager was a short, fat individual, already balding into his early thirties. Wearing one of his signature ill-fitting sweat stained shirts and baggy suit trousers with old worn trainers. Despised on the cluttered floor of the office block which he tried to rule with an iron fist for his superiors higher in the corporate ladder. Cyril was his favoured victim and target for the constant statistical abuse which is a common occurrence in all settings such as his.

After collecting the customary morning coffee from the staffroom, he slowly made his way to his desk.
The worn dusty desk was situated under one of the many uncleaned windows which looked out over the small urban sprawl of Chichester. At this desk he had to complete the task of filing records for a larger company which dealt in law. Boring and monotonous but strangely therapeutic was his job and for a comfortable wage which was neither excessive nor meagre

he got comfortably by.

The seconds seemed like hours as the day passed by, the only sound being the 'click, click' of keyboards and the occasional murmur of some nearby office gossip or someone mistyping and swearing in that traditional English way.

"Good afternoon"
The sudden voice jolted Cyril who was fully engrossed in his mundane work. He turned around quickly wondering who it was and to his amazement it was a pretty woman around the same age as him, she had golden coloured plaited hair and deep green eyes set into a perfectly smooth and well-shaped face. He could smell her sweet perfume. It took him a few moments to reply.
"Uh.... hello, how can I help you?" he spluttered.
"I'm new here and can't find my desk, it is number sixty-two. Could you point me in the right direction?" she said politely.
Her accent suggested that she was from the local area.
"Of course," Cyril replied, "Sixty-two is five desks down the aisle, on the left."
"Thank you" she said, with a gentle smile and began walking towards the desk Cyril alluded too.

Cyril began to think, she seemed strange to him, her smile, her way of speaking and mannerisms. But after a fleeting moment of thought he went back to his tiresome work.

A glance at the clock on the wall behind him showed that it was finally time to go home. The evening sun still flooding through the murky window and onto the scratched desk. Pushing back on his chair and quickly rising he gathered his small collection of items which included his mobile phone, car keys and water bottle and quickly made his way to the stairs for his escape from the depressing building.

The concrete stairs, cracking under years of neglect twisted their way to the front lobby and the portal looking front door and the car park outside which was miraged in heat haze even in the early evening. As he stepped out of the air-conditioned lobby and into the baking hot car park, he saw the woman who spoke to him earlier in the day. She was getting into the back of an immaculate sedan car which had tinted windows.

He stood and watched the car leave and as it drove past him, he got the primordial sense that someone was watching him from the vehicle.

Getting to his car he put his things away and then a spur of the moment decision made him

decide to go into the city to get some shopping.
He was fed up of eating the same freezer food
that he always ate after work due to his
tiredness and subsequent laziness. He wanted
something new to eat.

A quick walk through the carpark led him down
a tight twitten, hemmed in by thick flint walls
common to the Sussex Downs and used
extensively in the building of Sussex
architecture. Following the ancient Roman and
Medieval contours of the city he passed through
the reconstructed wall which was originally
built nearly two thousand years ago reaching
the cross shaped centre.
The market cross stood in the centre flanked by
the cathedral and main road on one side and the
shopping area on the other. It was bedecked in
Christian motifs and had worn stone seats
crowded with people trying to escape the
evening sun. Chatting and socialising amongst
themselves.
The shops were still open and bustling with
people. The streets heaving. Couples walking
hand in hand, families and groups of students
all filtering through the streets.

Wandering up east street he heard a shout and
then a loud commotion as a group of people in
front of him bolted to the left. He couldn't make

out what was being said over the ambient noise of the busy streets. A few more steps through the growing crowd he began to see what was going on. In front of him, kneeling in the middle of the cobbled street was a bedraggled, rough looking man. His hair was long and matted showing flecks of grey, his face looked grimy and unwashed with a stubbly beard covering his quivering jaw.

Cyril made his way to the front of the now rather large crowd which had grown to over two dozen people. The man began to shout and scream, pulling at his hair, clawing at his face and sobbing. Cyril got closer and could see that the man's clothes were worn and dirty. He believed that the man was homeless and most probably having some kind of mental breakdown due to drugs or some other kind of issue.

"HELP ME! HELP ME!" the man began screaming, tears running down his face like two gushing rivers.

"They're following me everywhere, make them leave... they attack me in my sleep. Please help me I can't take it anymore". After this outburst he began to shake and shiver violently.

At this moment Cyril, as well as most of the gathered crowd which was now gawking at the man in front of them, felt concerned with the welfare of the man.

Mobile phones were being used to ring for an ambulance but also some were being used to film the spectacle.

Cyril had the urge to help. He took a step closer to the man.

"It's all going to be alright. Tell me who is following you" said Cyril with hope that any answer could aid the paramedics when they arrived. The man with his hands clutching his dirty and tear drenched face went quiet very suddenly. Dead quiet.

The look he then darted towards Cyril startled him, it was almost if the man was staring right through him. His eyes bloodshot and red from the sobbing.

"The shadows follow me; they attack me in my sleep..." his pause brought about by the sudden remembrance of his nightly horrors.

"They don't say anything, they just follow and stare but they don't have eyes... but... I know they are watching me. Please help me." The man collapsed back into a heap of crying and murmuring after giving his short recollection.

The hum of sirens could be heard in the distance. The man began to wail again. Cyril moved closer and gestured to the man to take a seat on the pavement. Within a minute the blue flashing lights of an ambulance could be seen speeding towards the area at full speed. Driving onto the pedestrian precinct and forcing the people nonchalantly shopping out of the way. Cyril was relieved to see the ambulance approaching. Following close behind the ambulance were two black SUVs without number plates.

The crowd began to disperse once the ambulance was on the scene, some people still gawking in doorways or further away. Cyril was the only one left next to the man, thinking that he could help the paramedics by telling them the symptoms of the man's breakdown.

The paramedics clambered out of the front of the vehicle, one quickly moving to the back to open the rear doors and to get out a gurney to transport the man, the other paramedic walked towards Cyril.

"Is this the person having a breakdown?" asked the paramedic blankly.

"Yes, he has been here for abou..."

"Thank you we will take over from here, please go on your way" interjected the paramedic cutting Cyril short.

The black SUVs which now flanked either side of the ambulance came to a halt. Eight men burst out of them like lightning, all wearing black tactical armour much like the police but without the insignia, they carried assault rifles and sidearms as well as pepper spray, handcuffs and batons. On their sleeves was a strange symbol, a reverse 'L' with a line through the top quarter. They got in front of the sobbing man making a perimeter and forcing Cyril to take a few steps back. All of them had their identities obscured by helmets, glasses and balaclavas. One of the individuals walked towards Cyril, well-built and with his Assault rifle across his chest.

"Please move away from the area sir, this is a crime scene" he said

"Who are you?" replied Cyril confused, no crime had been committed so why was it a crime scene he thought.

"I won't ask you again, leave the vicinity or you will be put under arrest for a breach of the peace" said the officer, showing clear anger in his muffled voice.

"Okay, okay I'm going" Cyril knew if he had pushed further then trouble would have followed, he believed the police had become a law unto themselves in recent years.

The remnants of the crowd were now being shepherded away from the area by the other armed men, nobody dared argue back out of politeness or fear. A cordon began to be made with the iconic yellow tape, Cyril ducked under it and started making his way to the carpark. Looking back, he could see the man he had tried to help struggling while strapped to the gurney. Being moved towards the back of the ambulance, its wheels clacking on the cobbled street. The entire street was now locked down.

After a minute or two the ambulance sped off, followed closely by the anonymous SUV's, leaving the city centre and heading in the opposite direction of the hospital. The loud piercing noise of the sirens reverberated around the closed-in buildings of the city centre.

It was getting dark as he got back to his car and not as hot either. Driving home the roads seemed desolate and empty when they should have been busy, the sky became a mottled purple red and blue as the last specks of sunlight filtered away over the horizon, the moon and stars were quick to appear in all their glory and the unmistakeable sight of Jupiter and Saturn making their way across the horizon. Over the sound of the engine the faint sounds of owls, foxes and other creatures could be heard in the distance and the last of the bird song being whisked away into the darkness. Cyril thought himself lucky to live in such a beautiful and charming place. By the time he got home and did his normal routine of cooking and cleaning he went to his simple room and crashed onto his bed. Falling asleep as soon as his head hit the pillow.

<u>Chapter II</u>

The fizzle of the old, obsolete tube lighting which hung of the ceiling of the dank and mouldy tunnel guided the way for Private Anderson as he marched quickly down it. The incline so small that it couldn't be felt but every few paces was yet deeper under the ground. It was at this facility deep in the Wiltshire countryside where most of the important military decisions had been made for decades. The current situation being the worst they had faced since the Cold War. The concrete was cold and pleasant being so deep under the earth and away from the blaring sun above. Andersons' boots clicked as he reached the door into the next corridor. He knocked twice and gave the daily password; the air lock was broken and he stepped through the doorway into an identical corridor. This one was slightly shorter however and he could see the final doorway.

The guard asked for his pass card and identification which was standard procedure, Anderson happily complied. Staying silent and professional and after being given the all clear was allowed on his way. Wearing standard issue military fatigues and carrying a small black briefcase in which was extremely sensitive data about the current situation. On one of his sleeves was a small Union Jack and on the other was the symbol of the Internal Security, a small clandestine branch of the military which was kept secret from the general public at large. It provided covert operations for the military and secret service, and also conducted other operations which were deemed to be too 'illegal' for the general military such as psychological warfare. He had the common military short back and sides haircut which was a light brown colour and a hardened clean-shaven face with deep green eyes. He followed the military discipline to the letter and was mocked for it within his section.

The last door was very much like the rest but had both an electronic pin code and also a card swipe. It was made of solid steel like a bank vault door but smaller. He was quickly through that door and into a large room which was dark and smoke filled, a screen on the back wall flitted between photos of ill looking people in hospital wards and graphs and statistics of mortality rates and other depressing scenarios. Being as quiet as he could, Anderson walked to an empty seat at the back of the large table. It was surrounded by a dozen men of varying military rank, from the highest rank of General down to Captain. Anderson was the lowest rank in the room, being only a Private. The smoke

was nearly overpowering and stung his eyes.
The man next to him, his epaulette showing that
he was the rank of Lieutenant Colonel, offered
him a drink of a light-coloured substance he
deemed to be Cognac brandy. He politely
declined due to being a non-drinker and
continued to sit quietly watching the screen and
the information that was on it though the haze
of smoke.

It finished within five minutes and the lights
came back on in a blinding fashion. The dozen
men all turned on their chairs facing inwards to
the large and covered table which was strewn
with papers and photos.

"Well gentlemen, what is your course of action
on events?" said the General sat at the head of
the table.
"General Pierce, I suggest we do a mandatory
lockdown of the country and close the borders,
only allowing people in who have been tested to
see if they have any unknown pathogens in their
system. We could then determine what this
illness is and take further action accordingly"
replied another general.
"A good idea Sir, but what about the economic
destruction that would cause, it is dangerously
close to a depression and has been for decades.
A lockdown would cause more death and

misery than this so-called illness" said a
Colonel, who was happily dragging on a large
Cuban cigar. A silence fell on the room as they
all contemplated what just been said.

"Private Anderson, have you got the reports?"
said General Pierce
"Yes sir" replied Anderson
"Good, hand them over and help yourself to any
food or refreshments" said General Pierce.
Anderson passed over the briefcase before
sitting back down silently. The General looked
over the papers, reading them quickly and
making alarmed expressions at each of the
many bullet-points in front of him, his brow
furrowed.

"This is a disaster" He responded. Getting up
and placing the document under the projector
for the rest of the men to see. It showed a graph
which included an up to date mortality rate.
"Last night 600 people died of unknown causes
after suffering delirium and what medical
professionals have named as "Night Terror
Death Syndrome", there is no defined age group
it affects more, and the 600 people who passed
away were of different backgrounds. It also
included people who had underlying health
conditions and people who were seemingly

healthy. Most of them dying within 6 hours of onset of delirium. And even more surprisingly 75% of those who died, did so within an hour of dawn."
Stunned silence filled the room.

"Isn't there a bacterial, viral or even fungal cause to this? Possibly an undiscovered amoeba?" said a Colonel looking scared.
"The document says the medical professionals have done tests and have found no evidence of any viral, bacterial or fungal infections. Amoeba and prion disease have also been ruled out by autopsy" replied the General. Changing the slide to the next document which now showed a photo of the United Kingdom and all of the areas where the 600 people who died were located. Large red circles fixated on London, Birmingham, Bristol, Glasgow, Belfast, Manchester, Leeds, Newcastle, Brighton and Liverpool. With smaller and more sparsely located dots appearing in between the larger ones.
"These are the locations of all of the deceased from last night, as you can see the vast majority of those who had the illness are in built up metropolitan areas, with sparsely dotted individuals in more rural areas. 500 out of the 600 deceased were in urban areas with other 100 being in rural areas. Those investigating are

not sure if this is just coincidence or if it's because this illness is transmissible and urban areas housing more people leads to quicker spread. Investigations are still ongoing" continued General Pierce.

Anderson sat silently watching and listening, remembering everything said and all of the data being shown. Being a member of the Internal Security meant he was trusted; some members of the normal military branches wouldn't dare go against the Internal Security branch out of fear. Their reputation was well known.

The next slide the general showed was of hospital wards filled with bodies, there were even lifeless people laying on the floor of the wards, in-between the crammed beds and at the end of them. Doctors and nurses rushing around trying to tend to the sick while also trying not to trip over the struggling individuals lying on the cold tiled floor. Some of those patients were clearly already deceased with pale, lifeless expressions on their faces. Others were still fighting to survive, coughing and struggling. Sweat pouring of them and blood flowing from their eyes, nose, mouth, and ears. One middle aged man was struggling with a group of doctors trying to restrain him, grabbing his arms and clamping them to the metal bars of the bed. He was screaming manically but was restrained after a few seconds. The doctors all covered in hazmat suits, with large plastic masks over their faces. The men in the room watching such depressing scenes were all very familiar with the passing of life through their combined military past but the faces some of them pulled at seeing the video was that of pure, unfiltered horror.

The cameraman walked from that ward to the next, and the situation was much the same with patients piled up in the corridor, and in the next ward.

"This was the situation in one of the large London hospitals last night gentlemen, 98 individuals who were all transported there for treatment. None of them survived..."

"It won't be long before this gets out into the general public and mass panic ensues. I suggest we tell the media to report on it sparingly and claim it is a rare tropical disease of some kind. Get the medical professionals at Oxford, Cambridge and the Imperial College to make a statement claiming there is nothing to fear and everything is under complete control. The PM must make a small statement saying he has spoken to the medical community and they have assured him that there is nothing to be alarmed about. Do any of you have any further suggestions?". Genral Pierce was physically sweating and looked worn out, he reached into his pocket and pulled out a packet of cigarettes. Lighting one and filling the room once again with acrid smoke.

"I suggest we import a large supply of masks and other equipment for use in the event of a large spread or outbreak of this illness. And put the military on standby for use incase of breakdown of law and order. We should also tell the PM to have checkpoints in and out of London ready for use of a general lockdown of the country. If London collapses then the rest of the country will. It must be secured at all costs" replied a shrill Major General who wore a rat like moustache and a pair of worn spectacles which hung of his crooked nose.

"In the case of a general breakdown in order the military should be given full control over law enforcement and the government should be replaced by an interim military council who will restore order" he continued.

Anderson was not shocked at such a statement. He knew full well that the government wasn't free and elected. It was actually controlled by a small group of individuals in the military in which he was surrounded by in the small smoke- filled room.

He checked his watch and seeing it was now 19:50 he started to get ready to leave and go to

his next errand for Internal Security. He quietly
stood up and saluted the military seniors who
sat at the table. They saluted back.
"Thank you, Private Anderson" said General
Pierce while saluting.

He stepped out of the room and back into the
cold tunnel, the air was cleaner and he was
happy to get a breath of 'fresh' air. About as
fresh as recycled bunker air can be. Following
his footsteps back up to the higher levels, of the
base quickly and saluting the guards on each
door in proper military fashion. As he climbed
higher through the levels he could noticeably
feel the change in temperature from the cool
levels below him now becoming warmer and
warmer as he started to get to the surface.
There was also a larger amount of personnel,
mainly from the military intelligence, those who
work on electronic warfare and some other
normal personnel who were standard military.
They were mainly in the role of guarding secure
areas and doing patrols of the corridors.
Anderson noticed that many of the personnel
looked down or tried to pretend not to see him
when they saw his Internal Security patch.

He now reached the second level which was
composed of rows upon rows of rooms filled
with computers and individuals seated at them.

They were monitoring communications in the public. Every word typed and everything said out loud was recorded and stored in a vast database for future reference if needed. Anderson knew not even the Generals and the government were safe from such measures, Internal Security ran the data collection wing of the military and he knew that those who believed they had power would be blackmailed if they stepped out of line. He also knew they recorded his phone calls and text communications so he had to take measures to evade such practices.

It wasn't long before he reached the last level which was filled mostly with normal military types and non-military individuals doing the daily tasks of any military base. Many of them being trained in basic military intelligence. He got to the final doorway which led out of the main building and after being stopped and asked for his papers once again by a nervous looking Private who was obviously newly recruited into the Army. His hand physically shaking as he looked back and forth at Anderson and the ID card he carried. Anderson couldn't help but smirk, making the Private shake even more and a thin streak of perspiration cross his brow.
"Everything is ok you are clear to leave" croaked

the nervous Private in a high-pitched tone. "Thank you Private" replied Anderson still trying to hold back a laugh.

He allowed the automatic door to open and stepped outside into the blistering summer sun. The heat hit him like a wave, he longed for the end of summer and the cold embrace of winter. He began walking towards his billet at the edge of the base, happy in the knowledge of all the data he had collected from the meeting and the chance he could share it with his associates in the next few days. The sound of gunfire from the ranges resonated around the base, he knew after what he had heard in the meeting that the military was gearing up for something large and were getting their practice in before it was too late.

He reached his billet which was at the edge of the camp and quite luxurious for military standards. Built in the 1950s for officers and their aides it seemed dilapidated on the outside with bricks falling apart and the mortar in between them in serious need of maintenance. The inside was spaced out into a dozen separate rooms which all had an ensuite bathroom and cooking facilities. Since the beginning of the year they had been allocated to the dozen men of Internal Security in stark contrast to the

living quarters of the other military men on the
base who were usually crammed into prison
like blocks or shed like wards. The floors and
walls were tiled in the old style and the ceiling
was in the disgusting popcorn coating that was
also common during the billet's construction.
He wandered through the lobby area and down
a large dimly lit corridor which had six doors on
each side, his was number eleven. The doors all
had locks on the inside but not on the outside so
it was very easy for other members of the
Internal Security to snoop on each other, and
this was actively encouraged by the higher ups
in that branch of the military in order to purge
all those determined to be a threat to security
and secrecy. It was well known that those who
were found out to be a threat to the branch
usually disappeared and were never found.

He opened the door into his modest room. It
had a single bed, desk, a short passageway
leading to the en-suite bathroom and another
door next to the en-suite which led to the
miniscule garden at the back of the billet. His
various objects including his webbing and rifle
were in a corner, ready if needed at the pinch of
a button. His spare on-base attire was hanging
up in the cramped wardrobe. On the desk was a
small computer used to do administrative work
when not on other errands, he also used it to

play video games or watch movies when off duty which was very rare. A small space in the middle of the room was dedicated to his exercise regime, although there was a gym on the base, he didn't enjoy frequenting it due to the amount of unsavoury characters which decided to loiter within its walls. Before doing anything else he decided to boil the small kettle he had and made himself a drink, but also to create noise in order to make it more difficult for any listening devices in the room to hear him. He then went round the room, looking in any crevices for small microphones or cameras. After a few minutes he found a miniscule microphone hidden in the lampshade overhanging the room. He crushed it under his boot before flushing it down the toilet.

He did a second sweep of the room to be extra careful and didn't find anything else. The microphone was a cheap make and would be bad quality leading him to believe that one of his associates in the Internal Security planted it. He would eventually find out who placed it.

He would get a few hours rest before his next assignment later that night, which would include the surveillance of a few suspect individuals on the base. It was one of his favourite past times.

<u>Chapter III</u>

The darkness of early morning was cut by the bright glow of the waxing crescent moon. Shadows on the barren windswept grassy hill danced in the pale light, small bands of cirrus clouds moved in from the south.
The group gathered in the centre chatting in low voices. Twinkling lights far off in the distance brightened the horizon but the darkness was more numerous and more powerful. Not much further than the lights was the dead looking sea which reflected some moonlight. The quiet sleepy streets of Chichester the most visible and its cathedral spire looming up into the darkness like a knife. The hill they stood on being a gathering spot for their kind going back millennia. Being a site of Saxon Folkmoots, a Brittonic Druid meeting place and much further back a Neanderthal religious festival site, after a brief hiatus it was again being used.

The group of hooded and robed figures stopped chatting and began to form a ring. It was that hour in which it was the easiest to open the gateway. Their crimson coloured robes fluttered in the wind which had picked up. They all locked hands and slowly started moving clockwise. All that could now be heard was the movement of grass and the rustle of the wind.

A female in the group, her blonde hair cascading
out of her hood and falling beneath her breast
began to speak, her voice monotone but sweet
and also fanatic;
"We have congregated here like our ancestors
have for one-hundred generations and more,
our descendants will congregate here after us
for much more than that. The gateway is now
open after so much struggle and cannot be shut.
The Archons are amongst us and shall do their
work, the world will be purged and built anew.
We have begun the great work!"

In unison the group began chanting. The ring
they made getting quicker and quicker in its
movements. The robes they wore now
becoming like the clouds above them in shape.
After what seemed like an eternity they
suddenly stopped, falling to the ground in a
dizzy crash. Mentally and physically exhausted
they all lay on the grass looking to the sky. The
clouds had now vanished inland leaving only
the bright moon and the many thousands of
stars which spread across the sky in a vast and
deeply beautiful palette of celestial landscape
above them, with the hints of red and white of
the flickering stars and the darkness of the huge
dust clouds which obscured the centre of the
galaxy. Many constellations could be seen and
many stars which they were all familiar with.

Sirius, Arcturus, Rigal, Procyon, Fomalhaut and
many more.

Within this great sea of stars however a dark
void began to grow. It obscured the background
light of the heavens and even the light which
was coming of the moon. It started small and
barely visible but rapidly grew. After two
minutes it covered a section of sky around the
same size as the moon, however it was obvious t
was closer to earth than the moon. Clinging at
the edges of the atmosphere.
The group which was still lying on the cold
ground watched and waited in great
anticipation. They knew their great work was
done for a small while.
The black mass was still growing at an
exceptional rate, tendrils of darkness reaching
out in all directions and consuming a large
portion of the sky over the South Downs.
It then stopped within a few seconds, hanging in
the sky like a void of liquid obsidian. The entire
world seemed to go dead silent in these few
seconds. The distant sound of chirping
grasshoppers and a howling owl broke the
silence, the breeze began to pick up again being
whipped up the hill from the Solent.

A sound like thunder but many times louder
blasted from the void making all those gathered

on the hill jump slightly with fright and catch
their breath from the shockwave which hit
them. It contoured and turned, its edges ragged
and drawn out flexing and stretching. the sky
around it moving in unison much like a heat
shimmer on a hot road in summer. The group
was fixed, in awe at such a large gateway. They
had opened gateways before but never one this
large. They could see the darkness spilling out
from that realm into theirs, filtering into the sky
before disappearing into nothing like ash
floating up into the sky from a fire.

Then it was gone as quickly as it had come and
the stars it had blocked out reappeared in the
sky like milky dots on a dark canvas. The group
began to get up, their robes trailing around
them and being lashed about by the increased
wind. They were ecstatic at the completion of
one of their many tasks. Opening a gate to allow
in the darkest of darkness.

A fire was made in celebration and they began
to revel with supplies they had brought for the
occasion. They feasted and drank into the early
morning light before dispersing back to their
respective areas, waiting until the next occasion
called for their meeting. The morning light
appeared in the distance and the smouldering
fire began to die with lack of fuel. The last wisps

42

of smoke going up into the clear sky. A new age
had begun.

Chapter IV

Cyril's small bedroom was dark, just how he liked it, any background light would impede him falling asleep so everything had to be turned off. His old and outdated curtains were pulled across the small window and glowed with the low light of the moon which was beaming at this early hour in the morning. He was deeply asleep even after the stresses of the day, once he got to sleep, he was always difficult to wake being such a deep sleeper. The window was slightly ajar allowing a slight breeze into the room, cooling it down after the hot day before. His curtains fluttered slightly in the breeze, and the net behind them which was secured in order to stop mosquitos and other insects from entering his room.

He was laid on his back which was his favourite sleeping position and had pushed the heavy duvet nearly fully off the bed during his deep slumber. Although the room was cooler than it was during the day it was still hot enough to be uncomfortable. He was deep in the throes of REM sleep, his eyes flittering under their lids and his limbs moving slightly while he dreamt. He was dreaming of the day's events, of helping the distressed man and the police response afterwards, but this time it changed. The man

who was distressed didn't get taken away, he
began to change into a grotesque shape with
limbs much longer than any human could ever
have. His arms stretched down to the floor and
his neck began to grow longer before his head
finally flopped down onto his shoulder before
falling even below his shoulder and onto his
chest. All the while this was happening, he was
staring at Cyril and smiling, not a happy smile
but a sinister smile. Cyril began to feel terror as
this grim spectacle unfolded in front of him. He
looked around at the other people in the street
and they all either had their faces covered or
had no faces at all, instead they just had a flat
patch of skin where the face was supposed to
be. He felt entirely alone. Taking a few steps
back he tried to turn and run away but the man
was then in front of him when he turned, as if he
had teleported. He was now reared up,
supporting himself with his extra-long arms and
was slowly moving towards Cyril. Smiling all the
while. His eyes had turned entirely black and
began to leak down his face and dripped onto
the floor in front of him, like two pools of oil
which had replaced his eyes. Cyril fell
backwards unable to look away from the
monster. Its flopping head was getting close to
his and its eyes didn't move they stared straight
into him, he was stuck to the spot with fear.
It was only a few feet away when its smiling

mouth opened and rows upon rows of bristling teeth became visible, they were not like human teeth but more like that of a Lamprey or Great White Shark. He could still see it was smiling as its mouth opened and lurched forward like a predator towards him. Its cavernous mouth surrounding Cyril's head. The moment before its teeth touched Cyril's skin he woke up.

His eyes flashed open. The room was dark like he liked it but it didn't feel right to him. He tried to move his arms but they wouldn't work, and then his legs which had the same problem. Even his head wouldn't move, all that worked was his eyes. He was panicking now, sweat beaded on his brow and he could feel it sliding down his face.

Out of the darkness he saw movement, he thought it could have just been the breeze which was moving the curtains slightly but this movement was that of a person moving and not a breeze. It was too dark to identify who or what it was and he couldn't move his lips or tongue to speak. It was moving very slowly and gracefully, almost like it was floating instead of walking. It was making its way towards his bed, not going straight towards him but instead moving its way along the wall. As it crossed the threshold of the window portal, he glimpsed for a moment what it was. It was in the shape of a man, around 7ft tall and entirely made of darkness. It had no discernible features or clothing; it was just human shaped. He could sense that it was watching him and that its 'eyes' if it had any in that pitch-black darkness were staring into his soul. His body began to shiver, his fists clenched and unclenched in rapid succession, his teeth grinding in fear.

It silently crept around the side of the room and once it passed the window it disappeared back into the darkness. Cyril could see it in his peripheral vision moving in the darkness, before it stopped and stood still for a while, silently watching. It then began to creep forward in its floating manner. Getting to the side of the bed Cyril could now see most of it. It was just a black humanoid mass, through the fear which he was experiencing he tried to logically think, telling himself that he was just having a nightmare and he would wake up soon however the primordial and deep-set aspect of his fear was overpowering. All he wanted to do was run for his life but he couldn't move. The entity was above him now looking down on him, its arm began to lift slowly and a part of the darkness on the end of its arm, which Cyril discerned was a finger, moved towards him. It was pointing at his head and getting closer very slowly. As it got a few centimetres from him it changed into that of an open hand which was moving around his neck. Whatever this thing was it was trying to strangle him. Its hand closed around his neck and he could feel it slowly squeezing, his breathing reacted to it, with it becoming harder to exhale and inhale as each second passed.

It was at this time that the TV in his room began to flicker, it turned on and the screen turned to static. The noise added to his fear, with his sight being consumed by the entity and his hearing being assaulted with loud static. He believed he was going to die, wanting the fear and dread to end. He struggled and began to move his toes and fingers. The paralysis was wearing away, it was a few seconds before his head could move then his legs and arms. The entity had stopped in its tracks, its pointing appendage fading away back towards its side, releasing him from the stranglehold. Cyril sensed the entity move back slightly when he started to struggle free of his paralysis shackles.
He sat up in his bed with his fists rolled ready to throw punches at whatever it was, the fight response had now replaced that of the flight, his bed was drenched in a layer of sweat.

For a second the entity stood by the window

like a statue before it materialised into a black ball that stood around six feet off the floor. It was shifting in a viscous and gooey movement before it shot out of the slightly open window into the darkness of the night. Bolting upwards into the sky at a speed unconceivable to Cyril who only saw it flash towards the window as it went.

He was quickly out of the sweat soaked bed and ran to the window, looking out into the night he could see nothing naturally as it was the height of the night. All he could see were a few garden ornaments in his front yard and a shimmer from the paint of his car which had reflected some of the moon light which shone down from the twilight of the solar system.

"What on earth is happening" he whispered under his breath. As the adrenaline wore off and he became to think more clearly, he began to wonder what had just happened. He couldn't blame this on a simple nightmare, the being was clearly real and had manifested in his room but being the sceptical type, he tried to explain it some other way, maybe it was a hallucination of some kind, was someone playing a trick on him or was it a trick of the light. He knew deep down that he was just trying to cope with what he just saw.

Although he had experienced paranormal activity before and sometimes had become paralysed during sleep, he had never experienced anything as terrifying as this.

He even thought for a fleeting moment of calling the police but then asked himself what they would do. How would the police catch a phantom black shadow person? They would just laugh at him hysterically and might even refer him to some kind of mental health professionals. He decided on waiting until the morning.

He went or a shower and then walked down his creaking stairs into his small but practical kitchen to make himself some food. Crumpets with butter, a cup of English breakfast tea and some biscuits to go with them. At such an early hour there was nothing to watch on his TV so he decided to tidy his house until dawn came. His anxiety was at its highest level in years, worried that the entity would come back to finish him off, he kept on checking all the windows and doors were shut and locked.

He decided to put on the radio to listen to the hourly news, and to help him while he cleaned. He always preferred talk radio over music. The clock ticked down to four o'clock and the news

reporter appeared in the airwaves with his
rehearsed voice.
"Good Morning, I'm Donald Avery and this is the
four o'clock news. More reports of the strange
illness that is spread across the country this
morning. Medical professionals are urging for
calm and have told reporters that they will soon
have an explanation for the illness. The illness
which has claimed over one-hundred lives in
the past few days has led to spates of panic in
many of the nation's towns and cities, with
panic buying of goods and stockpiling becoming
an issue. Some local governments have enacted
rationing in order to stop the disorder."
Cyril was interested in developments of this
breaking situation, always being a follower of
global catastrophes. He turned the volume up a
bit more in order to hear it clearly.

"We spoke with local people in Woking
yesterday and asked them for their opinion on
the new illness".
"Hello sir, we would like to ask you your opinion
on this new illness that is quickly spreading
across the country. What are your thoughts and
feelings?" said the interviewer in a hollow, high
pitched voice.
"I don't hav' much time to think 'bout it to be
honest. As long as it don't hurt me or my family.
I'm sure the doctors will find a cure for it

somehow and life will go on as usual". said a local man being completely honest of his feelings.

The news then changed and the reporter asked a woman the same question. She sounded upper class and had the same bland received pronunciation accent as the reporter who was interviewing her.
"Well I am quite concerned personally; this illness could affect so many people and lead to so much suffering. The economy could faulter and then how will homeowners and business people be able to continue. It could turn into a complete shamble. I do hope it all blows over quickly and the doctors can find some kind of cure or vaccine for such an affliction. My thoughts and prayers are with everyone involved".
Cyril listened intensively to the conversations and thought to himself that they sounded very rehearsed.

After a few boring hours of cleaning daylight started to break over the horizon on another beautiful looking summer day in the rural Sussex countryside. Birdsong being the first sound to be heard as light flickered over the Downs as it destroyed the night.

Cyril was still shaken after the night's events. He was unable to take his mind off that dark spectre which loomed over him in bed, its image burned into his memory. With so much anxiety and stress he decided to take the day off work by claiming he had a bad stomach; this was a rare happening for Cyril who was proud of his record of not being absent for work in five years.

"I can't stay here. I have to go out" he said to himself. Pacing around the kitchen. He racked his brain thinking of things to do. He couldn't go and see any of his family or small circle of friends as they were all working. He decided, after thinking for a few minutes, to go on a long walk.

He wandered into his living room which was not as small as his bedroom and was filled with two sofas with a coffee table in between them. One wall was covered with a large bookcase filled with books of all kinds from non-fiction, fiction, books on art, history, science and much more. On the opposite wall was his Television and to the left of that was the old fireplace, with its tiled frontage showing it was from the Victorian age, it was seldom used since the introduction of heating, although he did use the mantlepiece to hold his clock and two candles which came in handy when power cuts affected the area which was frequent. On the floor was a worn and seemingly ancient Persian rug which Cyril was gifted when he first moved half a decade before by one of his aunts who he had only met a few times.

It was a short amount of time before he was ready to go out on his walk. He decided to wear his most casual and comfortable clothes which included a dark green woollen jumper, light blue jeans and a pair of worn out but extremely soft and comfortable walking boots.

He had always enjoyed walking since being a young boy, especially in the Downs which he was so familiar of, with its chalky slopes and wooded enclosures to explore. He decided he would walk the downs and then go into Chichester for tea later in the evening before walking back.

He set off just after dawn, traipsing through many fields and small woods, with a lot of the fields being left fallow or being inhabited with livestock of all kinds including cows, sheep and llamas. Sheep were the most common either on the slopes of the Downs. There were only a half dozen fields which included any kind of crop were visible. They were all corn fields, with their corn standing eight feet high. Cyril wasn't a farmer but knew from living a rural life that it was very nearly harvest time. He looked up at

could see a buzzard circling, looking for its
morning meal in the fields.

He began walking one of the many paths which
led up the Downs. It was chalky and slippery
under foot because of this but he marched on
under the now warm sun. The view was
magnificent at such a height, with the city down
below him in the distance and the water of the
channel far off behind the city twinkling in the
sunlight.

As he continued walking, he noticed that he
hadn't come into contact with a single soul on
his journey. He would usually walk past
multitudes of dog walkers on this path.

It was coming up to midday when he decided to
stop beside a small, fast flowing stream which
he knew very well, for a small rest. The water
was crystal clear and he put his hands in it,
enjoying the coldness. Over the sound of the
stream he could hear footsteps in the distance.
The unmistakeable sound of broken twigs and
moving foliage. As the person came closer, he
could hear the gentle sound of whistling. After
the peaceful sound of the stream and woods this
person sounded very loud in comparison.

A man walking relatively quickly, appeared
around the corner in front of him. Wearing a
beige shirt which had rolled up sleeves, green

cargo trousers which were tightly tucked into old and worn wellington boots. Looking at the man Cyril could see he had a round and pale face which was slightly red, and he was wearing a pair of old style round glasses.

"Good morning" said the man, slightly out of breath.
"Good morning" replied Cyril, "It's a fine day for a walk"
"Indeed it is my friend" said the man smiling. He was now only a few meters away from Cyril.
"The only inconvenience is that I seem to be lost, you wouldn't happen to know a pub by the name of The Golden Fox?"
"I know The Golden Fox very well; I'm walking that way so I'll show you where it is." said Cyril. He was quite surprised with himself as he usually kept his head down when speaking to strangers, being of the quiet type of people which are rare in the modern day.
"Thank you very much" said the wandering man.
They began walking in a staggered way as the footpath was narrow and overgrown. With bits of bramble sticking out of the hedges on ever side, catching their clothing occasionally. And long waist high grass here and there.
"Are you a local?" asked Cyril, trying to make small talk.

"Yes and no" chuckled the man, "I have lived in
many places, travelling is one of my hobbies. I'm
living near Guildford at the moment. I was born
in India my father worked there for the
government. I then moved to Burma for a while
before moving back to England and growing up
in Salisbury."
"Very interesting. Salisbury is a beautiful place
with lots of history" said Cyril. "I didn't get your
name, I'm Cyril".
"Robert Greene" said the man sticking his hand
out for a handshake.

Once the sun hit its maximum at noon walking
was almost unbearable. Walking through fields
was like walking through a desert with the heat
beating down on them. Woodland was a
welcome respite under the large canopies but
they were few and far between. The humidity
was also a constant problem and common to the
Albionic summer. Knowing cold refreshment
awaited them at the pub they kept up a good
pace down the narrow pathways which twisted
their way through the rural Downland and it
wasn't long before civilisation once again came
into view, with the muddy paths giving way to
concrete and tarmac, hedgerows replaced by
fence panels, barbed wire and chain-link. The
gentle sound of birdsong being replaced by the
dull thud of car and mower engines.

The Golden Fox came into view. It sat on the
edge of the main road with a few picnic tables
out the front covered from the sun with
parasols. The sign which fluttered outside was
that of a Fox with a Golden coat baring its teeth
while standing on a rock surrounded by
bracken. Another strange feature was that the
fox's eyes were coloured bright red.
"There's the Fox" said Cyril, wiping his brow of
the slight perspiration that had formed.
The building was Georgian in design, with its
symmetrical windows, two on the ground floor
and three on the first floor. It was painted a
clean white which seemed to shine in the sun.
Hanging baskets filled with an array of different
brightly coloured flowers which were dotted on
the outside of the pub, attracting a large horde
of bees which ignored Cyril and Robert as they
passed them entering the building.
The smell of beer and other alcoholic beverages
was nearly overpowering as they walked
through the old wooden door into the main bar.
"Now isn't that a welcome sight. I'll get us the
first round" said Robert.

The pub was lined with ancient oak beams
holding the ceiling and being further helped
with a few oak pillars around the bar. The bar
itself stretched the length of the room, being

covered in many mats to soak up spilt liquid and the pumps that lined it had a radiant glow to them. The furniture which was neatly placed around the room had a dark colour to it, Cyril guessed it was oak to match with the rest of the interior. The fireplace was unlit due to the time of the year and was surrounded by a few bookshelves.

At this time of day, the Fox was practically barren of life, with only the barman, an older gentleman known for his drinking habits in the village and another person who was sitting alone in the corner of the bar facing away from Cyril and Robert.

"What would you like to drink Cyril? I think I might have a try of their best bitter personally" said Robert, in his slightly eloquent but distinctively rural dialect.

"I'll have the same as what you are having" replied Cyril.

They walked over to an empty table and sat down. It was a table booth which was hidden from view of the bar. The wall next to it was covered in photos of the village through various different decades going back to the early 1900s.

Robert began speaking, making conversation, he only stopped to take small sips of his beer. Cyril sat and listened.

"It's been a strange week with all these people

falling ill. I'm very glad it hasn't affected this area too much. You would have thought in this modern age they would have a cure for any ailment."

"Some people think the medical industry have the cure for everything but are hiding it from the general public or only giving it to only the highest echelons of society. I don't know if theirs much truth in it though... a lot of rich and establishment people still get ill." Said Cyril, adding to the conversation.

Robert sat thinking for a moment while taking a sip of his beer. He then chuckled softly to himself before saying;

"There's more truth to conspiracy theories than people think my friend. Their's a slice of truth in every story."

His deep blue eyes almost glowing in the dim corner of the old pub.

Although Cyril believed this man was honest and trustworthy over the short amount of time in which he had known him he still felt as though there was something very sinister about him.

The time seemed to fly by as they sat chatting amongst the ancient walls of the Golden Fox, talking of local history and goings on, music, their family's and anything else that came to mind. After a few more pints of the dark bitter they were drinking it was after seven o'clock in the evening.

"You will have to excuse me for a minute, I just have to go to the loo" said Robert, getting up from his seat quickly and without much effort for a man who had drank nearly half a dozen pints of beer.

Cyril was suddenly on his own, sipping from the dregs of his beer. The room seemed to get cold quickly and he had a slight feeling of anxiety all of a sudden. The last drops of his dark liquid elixir tasted much sweeter than the rest, almost like someone had added a teaspoon of sugar into the liquid.

He sat back in his seat, relaxing for the first time in hours, closing his eyes for a few moments in contemplation. After a short time, he opened his eyes but didn't feel right. He had a cold sweat which rapidly spread over his body. He felt as if he wasn't in full control of his body, he tried to stand but didn't have any strength in his arms or legs. He collapsed back into the leather chair, expelling air from his lungs as he did so and then fell limp. He tried to call for help to the barman who was out of view but all that left his mouth was a slight whisper which even he had trouble hearing. He began to panic. It was like his earlier sleep episode but he hadn't slept, his mind flittered to reasons why it had happened, 'could it have been a stroke?' he thought to himself.

From his peripheral vision he saw movement. A dark shape was moving towards him from the furthest corner opposite his seat. Once the figure moved from his peripheral, he could see it was clearly a woman. Although his vision had begun to blur, he could see she was around his age and very beautiful, wearing a long red dress which flowed around her as she walked towards him. Her hair which flowed behind her and down to her elbows was golden coloured and shone as it caught the light above the bar, she got to within a few feet of him and then he could see her most impressive feature, two lapis lazuli coloured eyes which mesmerized him.

She stopped just in front of him, looking down from where she stood although she was of a petite height and didn't have to look down far. With a soft voice she started to speak, mesmerizing Cyril even more;

"You will come with me, do not fear, you won't be harmed if you comply. If you don't comply, I assure you that you will severely regret it."

He was in a shocked state of fear and he sensed that she could feel it. She smiled softly at him which didn't ease his terror.

He couldn't answer her request due to his
paralysis but he didn't have to because it was a
microsecond before he was lifted out of his seat
and following this woman out of the old pub.
He was being controlled, he didn't understand
how, his legs were moving without him telling
them to.

Outside there was a car waiting. A sedan that
was neither old or new, a steel colour with a few
scrapes and bumps in the paintwork. The back
windows being tinted a dark black, hiding the
occupants efficiently.
Robert was sat in the driver's seat not taking
much notice of Cyril as he was playing around
with the stereo trying to find his favourite radio
station. He stopped walking as he got to the
passenger seat and the strange woman opened
the door for him showing the dark interior of
the car. It was in an immaculate state, the
leather seats shining with LED lights overhead
adding to the ambience. Between the back seats
and the front seats was a telephone which was
strange to have in a car, being a relic of the past.

He clumsily clambered into the vehicle, half
falling before sitting upwards. He tried to turn
to look out the window but couldn't. He felt as if
his body was pinned to the seat as he sat bolt
upright looking at the seat in front.

His door closed with a bang before the front
passenger door opened and he saw the red
flowing dress of his captor climb into the seat.
While this happened, Robert had found his
favourite radio channel, it was playing classical
music. He could see out of the window from his
peripheral vision and he noticed that the street
seemed deathly quiet for the time of day. Not a
single person could be seen walking and
passing cars were few and far between.

"Ah damnit" the woman murmured to herself
before opening the car door and climbing back
out again. She walked around to the back of the
car and opened the boot and fumbled around
for something inside. Cyril was sweating
profusely, he genuinely thought they were going
to murder him.
She reappeared and opened car door holding
what was an old frayed burlap sack which she
preceded to put over his head very gently. It
covered his ears and eyes, blocking out all his
senses.

He could only feel the car moving. It twisted and
turned around bends and rarely stopped.
Muffled sounds of voices and classical music
added to the disorientation. At one stage he
could feel the vehicle travelling at high speed
before slowing down to a crawl. He tried to

make a mental picture of where he might be by remembering which way the car turned, where it stopped and where it started, it was to no avail however and he quickly gave up, especially when he felt the car go around a roundabout more than twelve times, making him feel physically sick.

The car was driving for hours. With the sun slowly going down and giving life to the stars once again. Robert drove and drove, through country lanes and motorways doubling back on himself and going driving to nowhere in particular. It was past midnight before he arrived at the destination they intended for, turning of the car lights and allowing only natural gloomy light to filter around them.

After the car had stopped Cyril sat in nervous horror. He waited and waited and finally the door opened and cold air hit his body. He felt tough hands grabbing his arms, lifiting him from the seat in the back of the cramped car, the stuffy air was replaced by the fresh cool night air. He could smell what he could only describe as the forest, that smell of petrichor.
Being carried he could hear the crunch of gravel under the feet of what he assumed was Robert. He tried to work out where he was, it was certainly somewhere inhabited due to the

gravel driveway under him, and definitely somewhere in the countryside.

He once again tried to speak and nothing came out. Moving his limbs was also fruitless but he could once again move his eyes which gave him some relief.

He was dropped down and then dragged through a narrow doorway, feeling the heels of his boots clip the doorframe. The smell of the forest replaced by the aroma of dried hay and mud. He was dragged a few feet before being spun around and placed forcibly in a chair which creaked under his weight and nearly broke. His arms and legs were tied to the chair and a further length of cord was put round his chest and secured to the fastenings on his arms, adding an extra degree of imprisonment. A hand reached up into his face-covering, tying a rag of cloth over his eyes before pulling the sack hood off entirely and tying another cord in his mouth creating a crude gag. He was relieved after being silenced in this way, logically thinking that the only reason they would gag him would be to stop him speaking meaning his voice will eventually come back.

His hearing was also back after having the head covering taken off and he could hear some muffled voices outside wherever he was and a few laughs.

The door slammed shut.

It was now silent and pitch black to Cyril. All he had was his thoughts of what could happen and why he had been kidnapped.
His legs and arms began to get a slight amount of feeling back and painful paraesthesia in his fingers and toes gave him a small amount of relief.

···

The small cottage was situated in deciduous woodland nestled away miles from the nearest settlement or main road. Made from local flint centuries ago, it looked beautiful. The windows and doors slightly ajar due to its age and the glass of the window cracked and repaired. It had a small barn connected to its western side and a large sprawling garden wrapped its way around the front and eastern side, it had a multitude of flowers from roses and tulips, daffodils, foxgloves, lavender, sunflowers and not taking into account the thousands of wild flowers which were dotted everywhere. Behind the cottage was a vegetable and herb garden, neatly spaced out and growing all of the common veg and herbs. The driveway curled of into the trees, being covered with a fine line of gravel, weeds sprouted wherever they could and parked in front of the cottage was a sedan. Moonlight glinted off its steel coloured exterior.

"We shouldn't be hasty in dealing with him Rebecca, I know you want answers but fear is the most effective tool we have. I could already sense he was near breaking point in the car when we left the village" said Robert.
He was sat at a long oak table which was crowned at the furthest end with a large open fire.
"I know what I need to do Robert" replied Rebecca, brushing her long blonde hair before slowly plaiting it into two golden bars. She was sitting at the opposite end of the table with her back to the fireplace.
The cottage was not large, it had an open floor plan on the ground floor which was dominated by the oak table. The sitting room was decorated in a rustic style with furniture which looked as if it had been there since the building was built. The middle of the building was home to the cast iron spiral staircase which led to the much smaller upstairs.
The upstairs was composed of two small box rooms which were used as very basic bedrooms. And a small bathroom, which still had its pristine bathtub which was installed with the house at its construction.
Floral wallpaper and dark colours were spread

around the house. Crimson being the favoured colour in the bedrooms. Candles and lamps added to the aura of the building, but made it cozy. With the light dancing on the walls from the flickering candles stirring primal feelings which still rested in the deepest recesses of the human brain.

The front door opened with a loud creaking and a man entered having to duck underneath the lintel due to his large height. He was built like a body builder and had a bowie knife on his belt. Although he looked like a brute he moved extremely gracefully across the room. He began making tea in the small kitchen behind the oak table, speaking in a quiet tone in his thick country accent.

"I've checked on him and he's asleep by the looks of it. I'll check again later on in the night. What's his name again?" he said.

"His name is Cyril. Just make sure he doesn't freeze to death tonight. It's supposed to get quite cold. We'll be waking him up just after dawn so I'll wake you up then Earl" replied Rebecca in a stern tone.

He just smiled and continued making tea.

Chapter V

The barracks was never this busy. Military personnel and hardware were being moved from their reserves and sent out to other parts of the country in preparation for something big. Lines of artillery were waiting on the main road out of the base, armoured fighting vehicles next to them with their engines running on idle. Men in full fighting gear marched to the parade ground to be assigned to their respective groups and be moved out to their objectives. It wasn't just this large base that was mobilising. Across the country the military had been put on standby by the government and reservists had been called up under the guise of 'aid workers' and told they were going to be helping with possible unrest.

Dozens of trucks were sat idling, with NCOs stood waiting to do a headcount of the men stationed with them. Men began filtering once called to their assigned truck and clambered in the back with difficultly due to the heavy bulk of their equipment, some had to be quickly helped by their comrades or would have fallen backwards onto the hard concrete.

Anderson was still in his room. Waiting for further orders and enjoying a morning brew of tea. He read the paper with a happy expression.

The main page showed pictures of burnt out buildings and people fighting with riot police in many urban areas across the country. People wanted answers to why so many people were getting sick and dropping dead. The government urged for calm but it fell on deaf ears. In London the largest amount of unrest for decades had occurred, with shops being looted and then torched. The Police fully losing control in that scenario and could only watch from a distance as chaos and anarchy ensued. Another article talked about how panic buying in the major cities was causing food shortages which were difficult to control since rioters and protestors were blocking roads and stopping food shipments from entering cities. All the mayor could do was ask for peace and reconciliation which once again fell on deaf ears.

The government had decided that it was time that the army was used to try and bring back order to the country at behest of the generals who worked behind them in the shadows. After a few pages of the paper was turned it went back to the usual talk of celebrities and pop culture. Anderson took a large sip of his drink before folding up the paper and launching it into the bin across the room, landing exactly where he wanted it to.

The sound of engines and shouting officers

reverberated around the small room as Anderson stood up and checked his equipment once again, making sure he didn't forget anything which would lead him getting a verbal beating from his superior officers in the Internal Security. His radio sat on the desk with its sound of static waiting to be broken with the sound of a command to Anderson. He imagined he would be sent back to London with his detachment to give protection to the elite who were now seemingly trapped within the city, although he knew there were many ways to escape that dreaded urban sprawl.

As he looked over his equipment and ticked off the small list he had created his radio beeped into life.
"Private Anderson, please make your way to the parade ground for briefing with Captain Jones. Bring all necessary equipment and be ready to receive orders. Over." The monotone voice went back to static. Anderson was glad he had his orders; the boredom was now over and work could begin.
He wrestled his equipment onto himself before grabbing his rifle, helmet and sidearm.
He exited his room, locking the door behind as usual and was met in the hallway by another member of Internal Security.
Private Bowyer was around the same height as

Anderson but much skinnier, he carried the same gear and was fumbling around trying to lock his door, dropping some of his equipment in the process in a haste to get to the parade ground.

Anderson could only smirk. Bowyer soon accompanied Anderson and they proceeded to quickly walk towards the parade ground, passing many soldiers who quickly averted their gaze after seeing their insignia. The walk wasn't that long although it was hampered by the huge build-up on all of the roads around the base. The sun shined down brightly on yet another hot summer day, wearing all the equipment they carried was an objective itself and many of the young privates in the army could be seen sitting alongside the road waiting for their orders to move out.

The parade ground was covered in people like a mound of ants swarming in groups to their designated assignments. Anderson waited for a few minutes with Bowyer in the queue which had formed. Once they got closer to the front a stout Sargeant recognised their insignia and quickly rushed them to the front sweating what seemed like buckets in the process through fear and the summer heat. They were quickly processed and told where to go by a nervous logistics member. The truck they were assigned to was on its own on the furthest side of the parade ground. Unlike the others it was not in the line of vehicles and stood out due to being avoided by the commotion of personnel.

Around the large truck was a group of men, some lounging smoking cigarettes and some others playing cards while sat on the ground. Their commanding officer was stood talking with the base commander. The two privates walked up to their CO and gave salutes in the standard practice.
The CO inspected their equipment and nodded approvingly, then the base commander made his way over and saluted them once again. They saluted back. The groups CO then motioned for the rest of the group to form up and stand at ease before giving his briefing.
"Now we are all here I will brief you on orders for the next twenty-four hours. Firstly, we have been assigned to the 12th Infantry Division which is going to be performing frontline peacekeeping operations in central London this evening, in cooperation with the police. Deadly forced is authorised however you will not interfere in what the 12th Division does. Any protestors wounded or arrested will be brought to a facility you will operate and be held under supervision." All the men stood silently, none showing any emotions, orders were orders.

"Any questions?" finished the CO.

One man put up his hand, his equipment jostling as he did so creating a clanking sound. The CO nodded towards him, allowing him to speak.

"How long will we be stationed in London sir". said the man in a thick northern accent.

"That is not known at this time, it will be at least a few days. You will given further instructions after twenty-four hours, unless things change dramatically".

The rest of the men stood silently.

"No more questions? good, collect your things and board the truck."

The men did as they were commanded, there was thirteen of them in total including the CO. Once they had all boarded the truck, they waited quietly as their CO talked in hushed tones to the base commander before standing to attention and saluting. He made his way around to the front of the vehicle and climbed in. Anderson noted that the CO had already stashed his equipment in the front of the vehicle and had squeezed in between it and the driver.

The truck was soon moving, crawling through the masses of men still waiting for their commands. The sound of the engine drowning out the few conversations that were occurring in the back of the vehicle. Anderson sat silently looking out and watching as they left the base and the bustle.

Dust was kicked up and obscured his view slightly. The road out of the base was flanked on both sides by large forests and marshland, with the stench of sulphur alluding to the latter. The track seemed like miles before they reached a main road and once they began their journey down such a road they were followed by two blacked out SUVs, Anderson concluded that these were secret service sent to protect their vehicle in the rare chance they get chased. A helicopter, very high up could also be seen following the vehicle.

The view of forest changed to farmland as they crept away from the base and closer to their objective. It wasn't long before they began to see large urban areas with their slabs of concrete sticking up out of the ground. It all seemed quite peaceful as they went through each urban zone, the only sign of unrest being the occasional piece of graffiti which would spout obscenities at the ruling elite or the police that served them. People were going about their business as usual, the only difference being a building or two burned out and a husk of its former self after a night of unrest.

Cities always depressed Anderson. He looked at
the urbanism which zoomed past as the truck
plodded on further and further into it and his
face dropped further and further. He had to
spend a large amount of time in the city during
his training in the Internal Security and was
glad to get out of it, and now he was back.

As they got closer to the centre of the city the
buildings built up more. With skyscrapers and
high-rise flats blocking out the sky. The whole
place seemed run down and decrepit even in
the summer sun. As they went off the main road
and down a smaller street which was a shortcut
to their objective a woman who was walking
towards them on the weed infested pavement
shouted some vulgar phrases at their truck as
they passed her.
The area was an industrial estate with factories
crowding the small road, all them closed due to
a curfew imposed by the local government. It
hoped by creating a curfew it would stop people
protesting, it seemed to do the opposite
however, by sending people home from work it
meant they had more time to go out at night and
join in the unrest. A semi quarantine due to the
new illness also allowed people more time to do
as they please.

The truck squeezed between buildings,

sometimes having to stop before going to a crawl as its mirrors scraped the brick walls of Victorian factory buildings, creating little clouds of brick dust which floated away. It then appeared at a main road and once again they were travelling at high speed towards their objective. They were only a few miles away and could already feel a change in the mood of the people. Graffiti and posters appeared more frequently, talking about 'power to the people' and 'answers' to the new illness. More police could be seen patrolling residential areas and loitering on street corners, looking for those who look suspicious.

Passing through another suburb Highstreet they saw a young man on the ground thrashing at a group of police who were trying to arrest him, he screamed slogans at them, trying to get up and run before being dragged back to the ground violently, people filtered past the spectacle with blank looks on their faces, some even got out mobile phones to record the arrest. Anderson looked out of the back of the truck with the same blank face as the people of the street.

They entered the centre of the city and were faced by hordes of police, in their high visibility jackets which made them look like a swarm of bees. A lone policeman tried to stop their vehicle before realising it was military, he quickly jumped onto the pavement and waved them past while looking like he had just seen a ghost. The large buildings which were mainly of Gothic architecture with the occasional steel and glass modern eyesore. Anderson looking closely at the rooftops of important buildings could see snipers and their spotters who were scanning the streets with binoculars looking for anyone who may be a threat to the status quo. The truck rumbled through the police blockade and reached its destination.

It had parked in an underground bay at a large hospital, crammed in amongst the cars of doctors and other workers.

Their CO climbed out the front before walking quickly to the back and dropping the tailgate, in the large expanse of the car park his footsteps echoed around the cave like structure.

The men got out of the truck in an orderly fashion before lining up and standing to attention. Their CO stood in front, waiting as a group of doctors could be seen getting out of an elevator and walking towards them. This group were all wearing white surgical gowns and masks which obscured their faces. Some even wore plastic masks which resembled welders' masks.

The CO greeted them in civilian fashion with a handshake and a nod. They talked for a moment before the CO turned to his men;
"Men, this is Doctor Charles, head of tropical and infectious disease research in the UK. He is going to brief us on what is happening at the moment and show us to our residence and workstations."

The doctors began to walk back to the elevator but instead took the stairs, the group of Internal Security followed them warily. The stairs led them further up and up for what seemed like a never-ending time. They finally reached the right floor and were slowly making their way through corridors surrounded by offices and laboratories, some rooms had dozens of masked people handling swabs and samples, doing tests on all kinds of horrible pathogens, some new some old. The thirteen men struggled down the corridor carrying their equipment, the CO at the back giving them shouts of encouragement or scolding them for slacking.
Anderson looked around collecting subtle details which he could relay to his comrades in the future, he noticed they were in a ward known as E7 and guessing from what was happening in the many laboratories he deduced that the E stood for 'Experimentation'.
A large automatic door stood in their way;

Doctor Charles typed in his code allowing the doors to swing open. They were faced with a corridor that looked very much the same but the rooms were filled with patients, some who looked dead, some others were struggling in their beds. Fighting against restraints, screaming like banshees.

"These people came in last night, a few hundred in total. Many of them have deteriorated in a space of a few hours, while others are still fighting whatever this illness is. We have some facts which are certain now though, one of which is the illness cannot be spread from human to human, we have collected samples of all bodily fluids and they are normal in every patient we have. Secondly, this illness is neurological in nature, patients have all got stable and normal internal function, however on examination of the brain after death there is a clear sign of grey matter deterioration. I've never seen anything like it." The anxiety in Doctor Charles' voice was plain to everyone listening. Anderson could see nervousness flashing across the faces of his comrades and the other medical professionals.
Walking past one room a patient had broken free of his bonds and tried to run at the door, crashing into it like a battering ram and causing it to jolt and set off an alarm. The group stopped

and two of the men in their group rushed to the door, holding it shut before a large party of male nurses rushed to the scene in full medical equipment and holding restraining tools. They burst back into the room, clattering the patient to the ground and restraining him.

They came to the end of the corridor and the last room. Doctor Charles unlocking it with a large set of keys he had fished out of the deep pockets on his gown. Walking in and turning on the lights showed a bare and near empty room which housed a selection of bunk beds. Kitchen facilities and other rooms which would house the bathrooms. Lockers were spread across one wall for their equipment.

"I hope you can all have a small rest before starting tonight. I have been told by some senior officials that you will be observing recently arrived patients?" said the Doctor.
"Indeed we will, we will just be taking some notes and possibly some samples for the military. Just do as you would usually do Doctor." answered their CO.
He nodded before leaving with his entourage.

Anderson placed his things in his assigned locker and chose his bed. Had a small wash and something to eat, his food of choice was a ration

pack. He didn't trust eating the hospital food.
They had arrived in the afternoon and it wasn't
long before evening arrived. It was decided by
their officer that nine of them would stay at the
hospital and observe patients while the other
four would go out on the streets and observe
what was going on and select individuals to be
sent to the hospital. Anderson was chosen to go
out with Bowyer and two others named Smith
and Walsh. They were all privates apart from
Walsh who was a Lance Corporal and so in
command of their excursion. They were all told
to stay with members of the 12th Division and
to not get separated. They would be carrying
their lightweight equipment, which included
their helmet, webbing and rifle. Anderson was
nervous, although not as nervous as his
comrades in the group. Smith was visibly
shaking at the thought of frontline action while
Bowyer was very quiet. Walsh was the only one
who wasn't nervous. He was a veteran of the
invasion of Iraq and had seen frontline action in
that war so he was well prepared.

The men were given an escort out of the maze-
like building. They waited by their truck for a
police escort to take them to a staging point of
the 12th Division, the streets were already
heaving with people, mostly young but some
middle-aged mixed within their ranks. Most of

them wore some kind of face covering to stop their identification being compromised by the many cameras and face recognition tools that the law enforcement used. Some carried placards with the same slogans which were carried on graffiti that seemed to be everywhere, not a single wall or building seemed to be free of the swirling letters and colours. The evening had only just started and it seemed peaceful at that time, with only a few scuffles breaking out and being ended quickly when snatch squads burst through the crowd, taking the agitators away.

The police van which carried the four men made its way to the meeting place in record time and without any stoppages.
The meeting place was a small square behind the police lines, it was green and pleasant with trees hugging the sides and flowers dispersed between them.

Commands were being shouted over the din of boots on the ground. The small detachment of Internal Security was allocated to the reserve of the division who were protecting two blocks in the centre of the city. They walked down the sides of the street peering around alleyways and keeping an eye on rooftops.
In the distance the sound of chanting and

shouts could be heard, getting closer with every passing second. Many of the regular infantry they were posted with were only teenagers, recruited from the army cadets with promises of good pay and benefits due to a shortage of new recruits which had been a constant problem for the military for decades. They looked nervous and some were looking back behind them almost as if they were thinking of running. Anderson thought if anything went wrong that evening then it would end badly.

They got to the junction and were told to hold position. Anderson and the other three men all stopped, checking their rifles and making sure they were on safety before holding. They each took a sip of water while they waited.

The smell of smoke drifted across them as they crouched, waiting for orders. The noise levels a few blocks away had also increased.
"Guess the riots started then boys." said Walsh, chuckling to himself almost demonically. A group of civilians trying to make a run for it down their road but were quickly told to turn back. One overzealous private pointed his rifle at them in order to scare them away but only inflamed their anger. Violent words being thrown their way before the civilians made their way back from where they came.

"Police cordon has been broken, repeat, Police cordon has been broken. Military moving in and using non-lethal means to disperse crowd." whispered over the radio in a sea of static and background noise.
The commander of the reserve detachment ordered them down the road towards the main ruckus. They were jogging as fast as their equipment would allow them. Anderson noticed people looking precariously out of upper windows of buildings out of fear or more likely pure human curiosity.

They soon reached the area of concern and waited once again. Water cannons blocked their view but they could hear a large struggle was occurring and objects were hitting the metal of the large blue machines which were belching out gallons upon gallons of water.

From the rooftops above some rioters had gained access and were now raining down masonry from above like thunderbolts.
Anderson watching closely knew things were going to get worse. He ran to Walsh shouting;
"They're on the buildings above us, you have to relay to the frontline that they need to pull back or they are going to be surrounded"
"I can't do anything; we are under jurisdiction

of the 12th Division and have to follow their orders." replied Walsh in a stern tone. Anderson just nodded and continued following orders. Over the radio frantic shouts and replies could be heard, some screams of people who had been beaten, maced or shot with water.

A large chunk of thrown brick tumbled through the air and hit a soldier who was preoccupied by the frontal assault. Smashing him in the head and shoulder and rendering him completely unconscious. He fell to the ground like a sack of potatoes, the crowd were upon him in an instant, tearing his weapon away from him and most of his equipment. It took more than a minute for the frontline to be rebuilt and repel the rioters who had a new sense of victory. The unconscious soldier was dragged away towards the group of Internal Security. Walsh made his way over and told paramedics where to send the man, they tried to disagree but he told them it was military business before they relented.

Suddenly a flash of light burst in front of them, one of the water cannons had been hit by a projectile and burst into flames, the fire consuming the entirety of the vehicle and dripping underneath. The heat from the flames reaching Anderson and making him put his

gloved hand in front of his face to stop it from
being burned.
Walsh was on the radio frantically responding
to the commanding officer.
"We have a green light, weapons hot. Wound
first but if needed then light them up" he said
over the intercom. Anderson nodded, while the
other two privates had stunned looks on their
faces.

The crowd which numbered thousands began to
make its way towards them. Chasing after the
fleeing soldiers. Some of them being caught and
dragged to the crowd and disappearing like
rocks under a wave. The first crackles of gunfire
could be heard. And screams as people were
being hit by hot lead. Anderson aimed at the
roof and pulled the trigger, in less than a blink
of an eye the masonry thrower on the roof had
collapsed from view, the group behind him
ducking for cover. Walsh let off a few bursts into
the air, a warning to the crowd who had broken
off and run in different directions at the sound.
A crippled and crying private was crawling back
towards the small group of Internal Security, his
face tinged black and blue due to the beating he
had endured from the crowd. His leg bent
backwards and pointing the wrong way, the
bone snapped and able to be seen poking out of
his trouser leg which was soaked in blood and

dripping in a line behind him.

The crowd was dispersed but could be seen regrouping further down the road, the anger of them clear to see and hear.

"HELP ME! HELP ME!" screamed the wounded man.
Walsh and Anderson rushing towards him and lifting him up. Another chorus of screams bursting through.
"Put him down in this doorway Anderson, he'll need morphine and dressings for his wound. You two keep us cover while we work on him. If anyone gets past that fire then light them up, is that clear?" said Walsh, his years in the army showed their usefulness at such a stressful time. The two privates could only nod in agreement, quickly turning around and scanning for anyone or anything that looked dangerous.

Anderson opened his first aid kit and found the morphine placed inside, injecting into the man's unbroken leg before tearing the trouser of his other destroyed leg. It showed a hideous sight, making Anderson wrench at the sight of it. He used the ripped piece of fabric as a makeshift tourniquet, stemming the blood flow somewhat. The man had calmed down slightly now he was under the intoxicating effect of morphine. He

twitched slightly from shock; his eyes closed.
Walsh radioed for medics and they arrived with
a stretcher, taking the young man away.
Anderson felt like he was in shock himself after
such a disturbing event but he continued almost
like he was possessed.

The crowd was coming up the road again, the
flickering of the burnt vehicle making beautiful
patterns on the shop windows and stonework
of the old buildings lining the street.

The group began edging their way backwards
towards the reformed line of infantry behind
them. Small bits of brick and bottles began
raining down all around them before a shot
rang out hitting Bowyer in the face before
ricocheting off Andersons helmet and causing
him to fall to the ground.
"Friendly down." Walsh screamed over the
radio, he kneeled over the lifeless body. Looking
for signs of life, there was none.
"Back now, run" he shouted at the two other
men. Bowyer now a twitching heap of blood on
the floor.
The run to the reformed line was short but
hampered by the constant rain of brick and
bottles flying down onto them from the
rooftops. A second shot flew past Anderson
hitting the tarmac in front of his feet and

causing it to fly six feet into the air.
They filtered back through the camouflaged line
of men. running towards the mobile HQ, they
were given refreshments before the
commanding officer met them, a man named
Major-general Garnet.
He exited the HQ and walked down the steel
stairs in ancient looking riding boots which
made a clanking noise almost as loud as the
gunshots which could be heard in the distance.
"How is the war going gentlemen" he said in his
upper-class dialect, laughing sarcastically.
The anger in Walsh's face was plain to see.
"Not good sir, I just lost a private and had to
send another man off with his leg hanging out"
he said. Anderson and Smith stood silently but
were glad that Walsh had spoken out.
"I see. Well the situation is under control now
men" said Garnet. "I request you stay with my
HQ for the time being before going back to your
CO, I have been told what your orders are and
will tell my people to send who they can back to
the hospital".
Walsh looked defeated and sapped of energy.
Saluting before walking to the refreshments
area and lighting a cigarette. Smith burst into
tears once Garnet had gone back into the Mobile
HQ to continue his real-time wargaming.
Anderson was relieved, his adrenaline starting
to disperse. The floodgates had now opened and

he knew change was going to occur. He spoke a few words of encouragement to Smith who was now blubbing in a corner, before making his way over to Walsh and sitting down next to him. The two men didn't speak, the only sound being the shouts and screams mixed in with constant gunshots echoing down the long street.

Across the country news had spread of the bloody events that had occurred causing protests to become more violent and widespread. In other areas of London protestors had created autonomous zones and ransacked military checkpoints. Chaos and Anarchy ensued, shops and other businesses being looted. Before a group of thousands broke into museums, stealing or destroying thousands of ancient relics. Rival gangs who saw an advantage in the chaos took to the streets, exacting revenge on each other in episodes of extreme violence.
In America very much the same was happening, riots and disorder spreading to a new level that had never been seen. Once again autonomous zones being established and some groups even claiming it was another civil war.

As darkness spread over the world a new age had begun.

Chapter VI

The eternal darkness which clouded Cyril's vision disorientated him, he didn't know what time it was, if he had fallen asleep of if he was dreaming. He could hear birds singing outside so made a guess that it was either dawn or dusk and knew he wasn't dreaming because he could move his arms and legs, albeit painfully. This fact gave him some comfort, whatever drug he was given had worn off and he wasn't going to be permanently paralysed. The thought of paralysis to him seemed more terrifying than the prospect of being killed and left in the dirty, damp undergrowth to be eaten away by worms and other insects.

The wooden door of the shed creaked scaring Cyril and making him tense up. He was waiting to be beaten or harmed in some other way. Silence fell over the room. He then heard something move and within a split second he was hit by a cascade of freezing cold water which made him lurch in his seat and lose his breath. His body began shivering immediately and he tried to breathe in laborious heaving gulps which made him sound like a stressed duck.

"Are you awake Cyril?" said Robert. He sounded slightly concerned.

"Ye... Yes" replied Cyril, struggling to get enough air in to speak.

"Good. Don't panic, I'm about to undo your binds and take off your blindfold. If you do anything, I'll have to deal with you" said Robert. Cyril didn't want to know how he would be dealt with if he tried to escape but from the sound of his voice, he could understand that it would probably mean him being buried somewhere quiet and secluded.

His wrists started to become free as Robert cut the rope binding them, moving his fingers caused loops of pain to run up his arms, he didn't know how he was going to stand after being sat down for so long. His blindfold was removed last as he was still sat in the chair. The light which filtered through the open door hurt his eyes, making them blurry.

Robert stood in front of him wearing his customary attire but unlike the day before he wore a pair of waders.

"I assume your quite thirsty and hungry. We are about to have breakfast if you'd like to join us" he said.

Cyril blankly stared, he didn't know what to do or say. Wondering if he had lost his mind.

Robert was stood waiting for him to get up.

"Come on I'll help you up" said Robert, holding his hand out, Cyril took it and was stood up. He nearly fell, catching himself on the chair and got a terrible feeling of dizziness and his vision darkened before going back to normal.

Robert began walking out of the shed and Cyril followed hesitantly keeping a distance between them. He saw the forests surrounding the small cottage, the flowers blooming all around. Even at this time of extreme anxiety he saw the beauty in the area.

He got to the cottage and the large wooden door was open, he noticed the intricate and exquisite iron fittings over the front of it. It reminded him off old paintings of Medieval castle doors, and although he knew it couldn't be that old he certainly knew it was relatively old.

He walked into the building and through to the main room with the large table and fireplace. There was no one else there apart from Robert who had begun setting the table and making food of some description which Cyril couldn't see.
"Please take a seat Cyril, I'll make you some food. Do you want something to drink, water? Tea or Coffee?" said Robert.
"Uhh... Uh, can I have a cup of tea... please" said Cyril stuttering.
He sat down opposite the fireplace, scanning

the room. The house just seemed normal to him. Not the sort of place a group of kidnappers would live in, he expected to be in a dirty grimy warehouse somewhere with a video camera set up in front of him and a kidnapper telling him to read a script for the media.

The smell of bacon wafted from the stove and made Cyril's stomach grumble in pain. Robert whistled a tune to himself, waiting for the kettle to boil on the stove before pouring it into the china cups. It wasn't long before he brought the food and drink to the table, placing Cyril's down first before sitting down himself. Cyril stared at the bacon sandwich, not moving or making a sound. He wondered if this was all a trick, was it poisoned or spiked with some drug. He looked up at Robert who was happily scoffing his own sandwich before stopping.
"What's wrong, aren't you hungry?" said Robert wiping his mouth.
"How do I know you haven't poisoned the food" replied Cyril.
"Why would I poison it? If I or my associates wanted you gone then we would have done it already. You would be at the bottom of the ocean with a block tied to your leg or would have had an acid bath" said Robert before tucking back into his sandwich with renewed vigour.

Cyril nibbled at the sandwich, waiting for a few minutes before nibbling again, constantly waiting for himself to drop down dead. He sipped the tea in the same way, trying to work out if it tasted strange or not. Robert sat trying not to laugh.

"What do you want from me?" said Cyril bluntly. The question took Robert by surprise as he took a large sip of his cup of tea before answering. "At the moment you just have to cooperate, we have no plans on harming you however if you don't cooperate that will change, and I guarantee you don't want that to happen. Rebecca will tell you everything when she gets back".

Cyril went silent again.

As they waited for Rebecca to return, they talked and Cyril read the paper. It was bedecked with photos and articles of people who had died from the illness. And more strikingly photos of what looked like a warzone in the middle of the capital. Bloodied bodies of people lying in the middle of the street, burning buildings and vehicles in the background in a scene of complete carnage. Accompanying photos showed similar destruction and anarchy across the country. Cyril was shocked as he read it. 'How could so much change in one night?' he thought to himself.

"The whole world is collapsing" blurted out
Robert.

"It definitely seems like it" said Cyril, he turned
the page and once again more articles on the
preceding night and others on protests in
Europe and America which ended in the same
manner with widespread disorder, violence,
rioting and death. Another article talked about
the state of the economy which had almost
crashed due to the uncertainty around the
illness and the violence. If it continued then the
currencies of the world would be worthless.

As he continued reading the rag in front of him
the silver sedan car creeped its way up the
gravel driveway almost silently. It reached the
front door and Rebecca climbed out, she looked
elegant in one of her long flowing dresses and
plaits. Followed by Earl who stood by the door.

She walked in catching Cyril by surprise. She
said nothing, just walked silently to the other
end of the table and sitting down stared at him
all the while with those large green hypnotic
eyes.

"Good morning Cyril, I don't think we have
become accustomed to each other yet, my name
is Rebecca and this little cottage you are in is my
home if you hadn't already guessed. You might
also be guessing why you are here and for what

purpose and I'll get onto that shortly. Firstly, I must ask you a question, do you see shadows when you sleep?" She let the question linger in the air for a moment, watching his every movement and facial expression.

Cyril was perplexed, he could tell she already knew his answer but didn't know how.

"Yes... I do sometimes, the last time it happened was a couple of days ago. It was the worst experience I've had since it began in childhood" he replied, trying to do as Robert said and cooperate.

"Good. When did these experiences begin for you?" said Rebecca. She still stared into him like an owl staring at its prey.

"I'm not sure, around five or six I would say for definite. My parents believed it was just nightmares or me being young and having imaginary friends. It would terrify me and still does but I did research and it is only my mind playing tricks on me".

He saw a slight smile crawl across Rebeccas' face at that last comment. It made him feel uncomfortable and he shifted in his seat.

"I understand how you feel Cyril but what you believe isn't correct, you've been lied to your entire life. What you experience during these terrifying experiences is real and I will tell you why bluntly. You have been chosen." Rebecca still looked for subtle expressions and

movements in Cyril, she could see him
becoming fidgety in his seat, a sure sign of
stress and anxiety. She would break him down
before building him up again as she wished.
Cyril only had stunned silence to answer for a
few seconds before timidly making a response;
"Bu... But they can't be real. Paranormal stuff
isn't real, can't be real. It's not proven by
science. You are going against years of data and
investigations" his face began to turn red, he felt
uncomfortable surrounded by so many people
who he believed were going to harm in some
way but he couldn't do anything.
"You believe everything you are told but yet you
don't do any research yourself. I know how
nervous you feel, your anxiety. It is quite clear
you are scared. I know everything about you
and more." Rebecca knew she had him wrapped
around her little finger now.
"You have been chosen by a species unknown to
most although many have seen them. They
appear during sleep or out of your peripheral
vision while you are doing some mundane task.
They hide in shadows and take the form of
shadows themselves although they can change
into any form if they need to. For thousands of
years a small group of us has been in contact
with them, especially on this small island we
call Albion. All the way back to the Palaeolithic
when they first made themselves known to our

species. Every few thousand years they would return to observe us, to improve a select few and meld their psychic powers. The ancient Druids and Seeresses of the Germanic peoples are two such groups who were given these powers. It was foretold that they would one day come back and reset the world in modern terms, once a vast portal was opened and their darkness could creep into our realm of reality. Only a select few are permitted to survive and continue how they please. Those that aren't chosen perish." She stopped for a moment, caching her breath and still watching Cyril who sat gawking at what he was being told.

"This illness which has just made itself known is one of the events which signifies their arrival. Soon the world will be wiped clean and begun anew. You have to join us Cyril, it is your only choice."

"Why was I chosen?" said Cyril dumbfounded.

"None of us know why we were chosen and we don't know if we will ever know in truth. Maybe it is just pure luck" replied Rebecca.

"What we do know is that a certain few people in society know about what is going on and are trying to stop the inevitable. They don't want to lose what they have built up, their materialism and control over the population. They have tried to create technology which will stop the coming of the Archons but none of it has worked. Now they can only wait for the coming collapse while trying to mislead the public with slogans and terms to calm them and reduce their fear."

"What you are saying is ludicrous, why would any of this happen? It's all conspiracy theories" said Cyril

"The man you saw in Chichester a few days ago, he was dying of the illness. You will soon learn the truth Cyril. You will see more truth than you can believe in the coming months, you will look back and know I was right." After she finished speaking, she stood up and beckoned Cyril to follow her, he followed and she led him into the back garden of the cottage. It was a beautiful garden filled with more flowers than Cyril had ever seen, trees and vegetables growing happily behind them at the back of the garden before the vast back drop of forest came into view. The garden wasn't ordered and neat like most but overgrown in parts which added to its charm. They stood on the patio at the back of the house, Rebecca turned to him before speaking again in her soft voice.

"I have been watching you for a while Cyril, years now. I know how you feel about life and how boring it is for you; I can change that. You only have to do one task for me. It is of great importance for you and us. You must go to a place and meet someone, an old woman who will tell you a few things. It might seem like gibberish when you do speak to her but that is not important, you will wake up once you speak to her." Rebecca walked into the garden and once again Cyril followed her, he felt almost entranced by her.

She picked a rose of one of the dozens which lined the grassy path. Moving it in between her fingers gracefully.

"You will meet the woman at the Devil's Humps at the date of the next new moon. In order for her to know that you are the one she is destined to meet you must walk through the Vale of Yews and be at the tumuli of the Devil's Humps at three o'clock in the morning. Do you understand?" Rebecca looked at him as she twiddled the rose bud in her fingers.

"Yes, I understand" replied Cyril.

"Good, you may stay with us tonight and tomorrow I will drop you off at your house so you can change into clean clothes. " Rebecca walked back to the cottage. Inside Robert was cooking on the stove, a stew pot was bubbling away and the smell made Cyril have hunger pangs again.

They sat down at the table and spoke. Cyril felt more comfortable and began to speak more freely with his supposed captors. They spoke of their backgrounds and childhoods, their hobbies and hates. He realised that Rebecca knew more about him than he thought, she had dug deep into his background over many years. They also realised they had a lot in common with each other, one of the hobbies they shared being Role-Playing Games. She showed him her collection of manuals and supplements, some more worn than others due to decades of use. He was enthralled.

It wasn't long before it was time to eat, the meal was served to the four individuals. Cyril still felt hesitant to eat after what happened to him the evening before, to reassure him Rebecca took a large spoonful of his stew and ate it in one gulp indicating it wasn't poisoned. He ate it with haste, his body exploding in satiation after such a long time without a large hot meal. He finished it and filled his bowl with a second helping. To the amusement of the other three at the table.

Night fell and the groups energy waned, they spoke until the late evening before they all retired to their sleeping quarters. Cyril had the prize of sleeping on the small sofa in the living room. His legs dangled over the end of the sofa but it was much more comfortable than his last sleeping arrangements. It took him a while to drift off, worried that the others in the house would do something to him or he would be attacked by the shadow entities again. His eyes slowly closed and he was soon asleep. Snoring gently.

...

He awoke in a fit, looking around at the empty room disgruntled and feeling groggy. He spotted a clock through dazed and blurry vision, its arms showing him it was half past six. Sitting up he felt dehydrated and looked towards the kitchen and being startled as Rebecca was sat at the table staring at him. He smiled;
"Good morning Rebecca, can I have a glass of water please?" he said.
"Of course," she replied, quickly finding a glass and filling it for him.
"We will be leaving in half an hour" she continued. Walking around him and up the stairs.

He sat around for the half an hour waiting, nervous at the simple task he had to do later that night. He was relieved as he could hear her trotting down the stairs before grabbing her keys off the table and motioning for him to follow her. Instead of her customary red dress, she instead wore a flowing purple dress and her hair flowed down her back freely. Being so light blonde, it shone like the sun in the morning sunlight.

The Sedan was beginning to heat up already and felt uncomfortable. Rebecca drove quickly along the overgrown country lanes which were dotted by fields and flint-built houses with thatched roofs. The roads were almost empty, and in the villages, they passed through not a soul was seen once again.

"Where is everyone?" Cyril asked, looking out the window.

"They're all hiding or dying. The illness is really spreading quickly now. Twenty-thousand died last night, across Europe over a million and countless more in the other areas of the world. We're lucky really, being in the countryside means we don't have to deal with the hordes" she seemed unconcerned with the chaos ensuing around them.

As they drove a few fly infested bodies laid on the pavement, in horrendous crooked positions. They had fallen and died as they fell it seemed, their faces contorted in a grimace of pain which was being eaten away by maggots quickly in the heat. Next to them were briefcases filled with money which having sprawled across the tarmac made the notes of money blow around in the breeze like snow. They had tried to hurry out of their house which was open with its door swinging slightly. Rebecca drove by not even noticing the gruesome spectacle, she was messing around with the radio trying to find a channel which had the news playing. Cyril was horrified, his face scrunched at the sight and trying to keep himself from being sick. The smell which emerged as they went past was as disgusting as the sight itself.

Rebecca found the right station and it began the constant stream of news, she turned the dial slightly and it became crystal clear.
"Breaking news for you now, London is being evacuated as tensions rise to historic levels again for another day of protests and violence. Flights out of London were suspended apart from those of important figures in the government and other important sectors of society. Fuel, food and water shortages abound in the city with taps and petrol pumps running dry and shops being looted for anything of value. A statement from the PM pleads for calm, order and thoughtfulness, however, most if not all of the protestors are ignoring the demands. Our reporter of the ground picked up on the situation."
The radio fluctuated between fuzzy and clear.
"...I'm on the ground here in London speaking with some protestors, they wish to stay anonymous so I won't say their names. Why are

you here protesting today sir?"
"I want answers, both of my parents and three
of my uncles have all died of this illness, they
took them away and I haven't seen them since.
How am I supposed to arrange the funerals? It
is a crime and the government is responsible"
the man was audibly distressed and they could
hear him trying to choke back tears in his voice.
In the background the chants of the crowd could
be heard and the smashing of glass.
"Here we have another protestor, excuse me
would you like to do an interview?"
"Yeah sure" said the protestor above the
ambient noise.
"Why are you at the protest today?"
"Many reasons, firstly because I'm sick of having
to put up with this regime in power, we need
answers about the shambles surrounding the
illness. I've personally lost two relatives in the
last week due to it. Another reason is due to the
tyrannical approach of using the army to
supress protests and then complain that people
are looting" the anger was plain in his voice.
"I see you are carrying some bags with you; did
you get these from one of the shops?" said the
reporter
"Yeah I took them. I see it as compensation"
replied the protestor.
Realising she was speaking with what would be
described as a criminal she quickly ended the

interview before returning the news to the studio.

"We wish to express the governments demands and plead with our listeners for calm, order and thoughtfulness. Please stay at home and follow the advice of your local law enforcement agencies."

Rebecca turned the radio off after the bulletin ended, not wanting to hear the drivel of modern music or advertisements. She drove effortlessly taking Cyril down a route he'd never seen before. He wondered if he was being conned again or if she was being serious.

Through forest and thicket, fields and hills between them they continued for ten minutes Cyril continued wondering where he was before the car pulled up to a junction and recognised it. A sigh of relief fell over him. He knew he would be home soon.

She pulled up outside his house at a speed, turning the engine off and turning to look at him with those emerald-like eyes.

"Do you remember what you have to do tonight?" her voice was full of seriousness.

"I do. I won't disappoint you" Cyril replied.

Rebecca nodded before turning the engine back on. He felt relieved as he stepped out the car and closed the door looking at his small but comfortable house. The car headed back the way it came and within a few seconds was gone from view down the old country lane.

His car still sat where it was left before his walk a few days before with a thin layer of pollen and dust coating the bodywork and windows. They had brought the harvest in during the last few days and nights causing plumes of dust to cling in the air. The noise of the tractors and combine harvesters in the fields all around, and the shouts of the farmers was not unusual for him. He had grown up around such work and even helped occasionally if he had the time. They were silent now however, which was strange as it was the perfect time for them to collect their produce.

The door was locked and he hunted for his key, an item which was given back to him the night before, he worried that his house was going to be in a state of disrepair, it was clear that the group had snooped around his house whilst he was kidnapped. The key snuggly fit the lock and he turned it slowly, trying to be as quiet as possible incase the door was boobytrapped or if there were any listening devices.
The creak sounded loud in the empty house, and once it opened his footsteps sounded like a beating drum on the laminate flooring of the

hallway.

The first thing he noticed was that the curtains and blinds were open on all of his windows, which he knew were closed when he left. He frantically began walking through the house trying to find other inconsistencies. Upstairs and downstairs he rushed around looking. He began unscrewing the lightbulbs looking for microphones and other bugging devices. Anything electronic was soon unscrewed and inspected before being placed back where it belongs.

It was noon before he was satisfied his house was cleared of anything that was planted. He ran himself a cold shower and put on a new set of clothes.

Studying the map for the quickest route to his destination was proving to be a challenge, he had a rough idea of where to go but his map was outdated and didn't show the location of the Devil's Humps. He decided in the end to go where he thought it was and make the rest of the way by torch light. Following the footpaths and tracks in the area.

Stories he had heard as a child of the area gave him an animosity towards it. Superstitions of ghosts of fallen warriors slain over a thousand years ago, headless horsemen and other evil spirits which haunted the ancient forests around and also the reason why it got its namesake, the Devil who was said to live amongst the barrows and hunt any who strayed into the area during certain important days of the year.

The clock ticked on incessantly, as the day dragged on Cyril tried to keep himself busy, tidying his house and doing some chores. Taking a nap before getting ready later that night. He decided to dress in more layers as it felt strangely cold. The stars coming out and cascading the darkness with light. Midnight past and he began to leave, getting into the old car which struggled to start. He wanted to be early, worried if he missed the deadline then he would himself end up dead.

He left and began to drive through the Sussex landscape, the headlights lighting up the hedgerows which had the glow of curious fox eyes glaring out. Further on he had to slow down due to a family of deer loitering in the road. A proud stag at the back following his group before stopping in the middle of the road and staring at the car, the antlers were the largest Cyril had ever seen. It hopped off with its group deep into the underbrush disappearing back into the darkness.

He continued onward and it wasn't long before

he reached the empty layby which was covered in foot high dried mud and shingle, he parked with some difficulty due to the mud before getting out, collecting his map, torch, phone and a knife. He began walking towards the area he believed the Devil's Humps were situated. He shone his torch this way and that at any small noises he heard. The torch would occasionally catch the glint of eyes peering out from under a bush or from around a tree, behind which a fox or badger would scamper away as he got closer to it down the footpath.

The woodland was thick and the light from his torch seemed to dissipate into the inky blackness. He kept stopping to check the trees, seeing if they were Yew or not. Most were Birch and Oak, much more common and numerous than the ancient Yews. He followed each footpath for a while before realising, he was going the wrong way, trying to study the map didn't help him much and it was almost by chance when he stumbled down an extremely overgrown path which was covered in a wall of brambles when he came across a large avenue of Yews which stretched into the distance. Some of them were on their side and growing weirdly, with their thick red branches growing crookedly upwards like a shield wall. Many dripped with their poisonous sap and their berries were

starting to form as the hot season came to a
close.

He followed them down and through a small
valley. He noticed the slight incline and thought
to himself "that must be the vale". The air was
getting colder and he was glad he brought his
jacket with him; his face could feel a gentle
breeze rising up through the valley.

He walked for a few minutes with the ancient
Yews going on for as far as the eye could see, he
reckoned that these trees were easily over a
thousand years old or maybe even more. They
may have been juvenile saplings long before
that, back to the times of the Druids and the
Roman occupation. He could see the end of the
treeline and a small empty meadow in front of
him, stepping out into the clear area the stars
once again became visible and the dark
silhouette of the moon which was in its darkest
lunar phase.

The grass of the meadow swayed with the
breeze, the crickets chirped happily and a few
moths attacked the light beam which extended
out of Cyril's torch. He stopped for a moment
getting his bearings. He recognised the area and
knew he was close to the Devil's Humps. He
quickly checked his watch and it showed him

that he had thirty minutes before the meeting time.
He quickly tucked him trousers into his boots because he worried about the ticks which would definitely inhabit such an area of which he faced at that moment.

He carried on walking through the waist high meadow, looking around for those three large bumps in the ground. It only took a few minutes before he saw them protruding from the ground, he wondered how many people had seen these majestic anomalies in the landscape which had been there since the Bronze Age. He expected to see the woman stood there waiting for him but it was all quiet and he was stood alone on top of the humps, checking his watch many times before looking up and observing the stars and pacing around trying to kill time.

It was at 2:59 when he heard some movement in the tree line, he turned around and shone the torch into the area but nothing was there. Turning of the torch he stood again waiting. He was about to walk off in frustration, turning around and almost falling off the side of the large Tumuli. The old woman was stood only a few feet away, hunched over a walking stick which stood over a foot taller than herself. Her wrinkled face covered by a frayed hood which would have been a bright purple a long time ago but was now a faded colour, almost grey in complexion. Her walking stick had many carvings on it, runic symbols which were cut into the wood and painted different colours of red, blue, gold and bronze. They shone in the night and he could see them much more clearly than her.

"Cyril, welcome to my abode, I have been told of your coming" her voice was as frayed as her clothing and Cyril could hear her lungs rattling in between breathes.
"I have a few things to tell you and I don't expect you to know the answer. We all know that our life is chased by death, it gets closer and closer every day, gaining a tiny fraction with every second that passes, but we all know that when death comes then the old life is replaced by the new. From decay springs forth new and more vigorous life" she stopped for a second catching her breathe once again, Cyril rolled what she had over his mind a few times, it was similar to what Rebecca had told him the day before.
"Great changes are occurring and when the next full moon gives way to the crescent then this dimension of life will be born anew. The light will be swallowed by the darkness before a new dawn is born. You will know Cyril."

As she finished speaking, he heard shouting
behind him, turning around to face the sound he
was confronted by nothing. Barren emptiness
was all that was there. He turned back to the old
woman and she was gone. He was left alone
once again on the cold tumuli.
He began walking back to his car, following the
same route he had come from. Under the
canopy of the Yews he felt that it seemed more
alive after the meeting with the old wise
woman. He was perplexed at how she had just
vanished but nothing surprised him after
everything he had gone through after the last
few days.

He drove back with little concern until he
arrived back at his house. The windows of his
house were lit up behind the pulled curtains,
someone was in his house. He opened the door
quietly and crept up to the front door, testing
the door handle which was unlocked. He
opened the front door a crack and peaked in,
the light was coming from the sitting room with
the rest of the house seemingly in darkness.

He opened the door fully trying not to let it
swing open with the breeze, holding his knife in
his pocket and ready to fight off any intruders.
He counted down from three in his head and at
one he jumped into the doorway, expecting to

see a burglar dressed in black and face covered
with a balaclava. He was shocked to find
Rebecca sat on his sofa with her feet up reading
a book with a steaming cup of tea next to her.
"Good evening Cyril, I heard you had a good
meeting with the old woman" she smiled at him,
before walking over to him and taking his hand.

They spent the night together.

<u>Chapter VII</u>

The hospital had the stench of bleach and other noxious chemicals which were lathered over every surface in sight. Sunlight broke through the shuttered window at the end of the corridor and bathed it in the soft glow of morning, the tiles turning a pale off-white colour.

Anderson had tried to sleep after getting back to the hospital the night before but it was nearly impossible for him, waking up constantly in fits and starts. Once he began to see the sun rising and the light filtering in to the bunk room he decided to get up. He ate some of the hated ration pack food and washed it down with black coffee before making his way out of the bunk room and to find his CO. He had heard quite a lot of movement outside his room in the night and now realised why. All of the furniture and other implements which had been situated in the corridor were gone, leaving only bare tiles and the lights hanging from the ceiling. Walking past office rooms and laboratories he saw that they also seemed ghostly quiet in comparison to the day before, with only a fraction of the staff working in them and much of their equipment gone. He reached the main office room which was being used as a makeshift HQ for the group of Internal Security and the doctors they worked with.

He lightly tapped on the door and it was opened by a young nurse whose eyes were bloodshot and her face bruised in the shape of the mask she had to wear for hours on end. The CO and main doctor were in deep debate with the rest of Internal Security, apart from Walsh who was still sleeping in the bunk room, stood behind their CO.

"I have had reports from my seniors that the hospital is at risk and to evacuate with all the relevant data you have collected and precede with us back to Government HQ. Your equipment has been seized by the Army and is being taken. The choice is yours Doctor."
The CO began to stand up to leave, with the doctor shaking his head.
"Fine. I will come but I cannot say the same about my staff. I will have to ask them all myself" replied the doctor sounding like he was going to cry.
"Very well doctor, you have an hour. I will meet you in the assembly area" said the CO.

The protests which had been occurring over the last few nights had now escalated to occur during the day, with twenty-four hours of constant vandalism and violence. Many areas of the country being abandoned to the apocalyptic like Anarchy.

A loud knock on the door stopped the debate and a young and petrified looking nurse walked in, out of breath and sweating.

"Doctor... rioters are breaking in" said the nurse, struggling for breath.

"Right, we need to move immediately. Doctor round up your staff and follow us down to the assembly point. Private Anderson, go and wake up Walsh and meet us downstairs." The CO was out of his chair and in the hallway in seconds.

Anderson after waiting for the rest of the individuals in the room leave left himself, walking quickly to the bunk room. Luckily for him Walsh was already awake and wiping his eyes of sleep.

"We've got to leave now Walsh; rioters are breaking their way into the hospital. I'll help you collect your things." Anderson moved over to Walsh's locker and began throwing him his camouflage fatigues and webbing before grabbing his own and putting it on. They could here muffled shouts and breaking glass coming from downstairs. This made Walsh get ready a lot quicker, they both grabbed their rifles and left them off safety.

Up the stairs the sound of dozens of footsteps could be heard, before long the first protestors could be seen making their way down the hallway, opening the wards and releasing the infected who could still walk. The few medical staff still left were trapped in their rooms with the infected. Terrible screams could be heard by the two men in the bunk room even with the door shut. Cyril opened it the slightest crack and could see people running past, but thankfully not taking notice of their location. Walsh was trying to silently slip on his combat boots, watching the door as he did so.

The sound of the screams, shouts and other heart wrenching noises seemed to dissipate as the looting horde made their way into the next section of the huge labyrinthine like hospital. They waited nervously for the last hint of noise before Anderson opened the door cautiously peeking his rifle barrel through the opening. His finger was ready on the trigger, waiting for the slightest amount of movement down the hallway.

Across the floor were scatterings of papers, x-ray images and other medical data which had been ransacked, windows separating the hallway from the wards were smashed and doors hung off their hinges, swinging slightly from the breeze coming from the smashed external windows which gave an amazing few over the city and the Thames which flowed slowly through it. It's water bobbing with rubbish and other debris, and a more macabre sight as a body bobbled its way along like a log.

Anderson scanned left and right as he left the room.
"Clear." he whispered as he went.
The first ward on the left was empty, the one on the right side of the hallway was filled with blood which had pooled on the floor and filled the cracks of the white washed tiles. A doctor lay on his back clutching his neck with glassy dead eyes staring at the ceiling. His formerly white lab coat was now stained in that scarlet glow of freshly dried blood. Walsh followed him scanning for what they in military fashion would call enemy combatants in a war situation, they didn't know if this was a war situation but knew it was one of survival. Stopping at the next ward Anderson dropped down and pulled out the small bayonet that was on his belt, putting it on the socket of his barrel with a satisfying click. Walsh copied him. The next ward showed more horrors. Six bodies of nurses, doctors and patients were lying in various parts of the room once again covered in the crimson elixir of life.

These unlucky souls were the ones who were left behind by the medical committee which had been taken by the Internal Security. Anderson pitied them.

They eventually got to the stairs and stopped for a moment, listening for any sign of activity in the floor below. They didn't take the lift due to a fear of opening onto a floor of protestors or infected.

They made their way down the stairs at speed, not bothering to check any of the other floors. Once they got to the bottom floor, they follow the painted signs for the car park, being more careful as they proceeded through the looted refreshments area. The lights above them began to flicker before going out one after another down the long stretch of corridor. They had no other option but to turn on their rifle mounted torches which lit up everything precariously.

They could now see the light of the large automatic front doors of the hospital which were opening and closing slowly as they lost power from the malfunctioned electrical supply.

Within the blink of an eye something large and metallic swung around an open-door hitting Anderson square in the chest and knocking him over. Winded he couldn't say anything and only watched as Walsh rushed to his aid. Spearing the individual on the end of his bayonet before he could swing the metal bar down on Andersons undefended face.

A groan expelled itself from the man's mouth as he turned on Walsh limply swinging the primitive club. Walsh pulled the bayonet out before plunging it back into the man's chest which severing a vital artery, made him kneel to the ground before pulling it out once again with a spurt of blood which hit the ceiling and narrowly missed Walsh. The man laid next to Anderson gargling his death rattle for a few moments before expiring. As his heartbeat stopped the spray of blood slowly subsided to a gentle trickle before stopping altogether. Anderson was covered in the warm liquid and tried to wipe some of it off on the dead man's clothes before picking up his rifle and checking to see if it was damaged from the fall.

"Thanks Walsh" he said quietly.

"No problem mate" Said Walsh.

They got to the front door peeking around the broken glass and seeing a group of protestors loitering in the road outside the hospital. Some of them were drinking copious amounts of looted alcohol. There was ten of them in total, all male and surrounded by a selection of items

but mostly alcohol and cigarette packets. One of
them opened another crate of beer, drinking a
bottle in one go before launching the now
empty bottle in the opposite direction up the
road, landing with a crash. They had a pile of
rubbish burning next to them in the middle of
the road which pumped out clouds of black
smoke from burning tyres and plastic and the
acrid smell was painful to the senses.

Anderson and Walsh wondered what to do,
Walsh saying they should make their way to the
back of the hospital and avoid further contact.
Anderson thought they should fire some shots
to scare away the looters before escaping down
an alley towards the main army cordon. They
both agreed that would be more dangerous
however due to being outnumbered and so
decided to follow Walsh's plan.

They struggled through the trashed lobby and
had difficulty finding the way back towards the
underground carpark which was the assembly
point, they knew already that their group would
have left. Their objective of evacuating the
medical staff and equipment much more
valuable than two lowly foots soldiers of the
state.

They kept low to the ground as they creeped

forward, turning their torches off if they heard even the slightest noise. Most of the noise was from creaking old pipes which ran above them on the ceiling.

They could soon feel cold air blowing from the underground carpark. Opening a blocked door which looked as it had been barricaded in haste by their comrades as they escaped and partially broken open by the looters trying to get to them. Their were also bullet holes in the door and a slick of blood leading off into a dark room. next to their exit. As Anderson broke the door open Walsh kept his muzzle trained on the dark room which was too large for his torch to light up fully. Whoever had been hit through the door had decided to crawl off into the room to die like an injured animal.

Anderson pried the door open with a struggle and after he and Walsh made their way through, he secured it again.
The carpark was empty as they imagined. The only things left being the empty cars of the hospital staff, a few bullet casings and ration pack containers.
Walsh sat down, head in hands.
"What do we do now? They left us in a hell zone surrounded by looters who want to kill us. The base is hours away by car."

"We have to get out of the city as a first objective, and we won't be able to get out in these clothes. We need to look like civvies. We can't take these rifles either so we'll have to ditch them. Only take what we can conceal." said Anderson. He began to take off his webbing and threw his helmet off. He removed his bayonet and put it back in its scabbard and kept his sidearm on his belt. Walsh copied him.

"We need a map as well, we need to head south, we'll get to the countryside quicker that way." Anderson ran over to one of the abandoned cars looking through the window with cupped hands, he tried the door handles carefully worried about setting off their alarms. He tried all of them, the second to last car being open. He looked through it but failed to find a map but found a coat hanger with luck and quickly made it into a makeshift door lock puller. With some help from Walsh who held the window open a fraction of an inch, Anderson slowly fed the coat hanger which had been pulled out straight and curled at the end to wrap around the door lock down towards it. With some finesse he caught it and pulled upwards opening the door. He got in and started rooting around, finding a small roadmap in the boot.

They decided on their route and also decided that once they got to the suburbs, they would have to find transport and fast.

The road outside the hospital carpark was abandoned, distant noise of disturbance and alarms echoed through the city, here and there debris could be seen. They kept to the side of the road, in the shadows and moved fast enough to not wear themselves out. They could see some abandoned terraced houses in the distance, modest accommodation for those who could afford it in such an affluent area of the city. Their former owners had left days ago in a hurry knowing what was awaiting them if they stayed. Some of them had been torched and were charred remains of buildings but a few still stood intact.

They crept into one of the intact Victorian terraces and lightly called out in the hallway to see if it was empty. There was no answer. "Right. You get some supplies from the kitchen and I'll go and get some clothes." said Anderson as he made his way up the stairs. It was a tiny house and only had two bedrooms and a small toilet upstairs. He walked into the bigger room of the two and found a large wardrobe filled with clothes. As he rummaged through a photo on the wall caught his eye. A large family sat in a garden, all smiling before any of this chaos happened. It made him reflect with sadness.

He collected some clothes of the relevent size for him and Walsh. Two pairs of Jeans, Two grey t-shirts and jumpers. Once they had got into the civilian clothes, they felt a lot more incognito. They continued to carry their belts however, concealed under their clothes. They headed out making their way southwards and further into the chaos.

Within a short time, they had walked a few blocks of the old city roads and could see a large crowd in the distance, as they walked, they drank some bottled water and ate some snacks which Walsh had found in the house. As they got closer to the crowd, they could tell it was more than just a few people, hundreds possibly thousands blocked the road. Music could be heard, laughs and shouts mixed in. A makeshift barrier had been constructed from pallets and rubble and graffiti abounded the area.

"Stop." shouted a whiny voice from behind the barricade. "You aren't coppers, are you?"
"No" replied Anderson
"Ok. Welcome to the Free zone, enjoy your stay." They looked at each other as they walked into the so-called Free zone. It was a crossroad covered in tents and ramshackle structures, oil drum firepits were everywhere spewing out disgusting smoke and music was blaring. The

people who inhabited the strange area were a mixture of local hoodlums and hippies, most if not all were on drugs or in the course of taking drugs. Some were so high they laid sprawled on the tarmac.

Music playing over speakers which were rigged up to one of the few buildings which still had power in the area and were blaring out senseless drivel at ear piercing volume.

Anderson treaded carefully, he was wary of used needles which could be lining the floor in such an area. A few stalls were set up selling cheap trinkets and junk food which many of the drugged youths were happily scoffing down in quantity, they paid by swapping drugs or cigarettes as money had become a worthless item. The waste oil trickled down the road and into the drain, mixing with the contents of a portable toilet which was leaking chemicals and human waste into the road. The stench was horrendous but the group didn't seem to care. They also saw some injured people laying in a makeshift medical area under a sheltered part of the pavement. Some of them covered in bandages and being given water, others in deathlier looking state and being harassed by fly's who were trying to get at their open wounds. Anderson imagined these people were injured trying to battle with the authorities and had come of worse from wear. There were always more people to replace them however.

A crazed looking man flaked away from the food stall and made his way towards Anderson and Walsh. Anderson started to move his hand around towards where his sidearm was pretending to itch his back just incase the crazed looking tramp tried anything. They both stopped as he walked towards them.
"Hey, you want some treats, I've got everything you need or want" said the tramp, in a wispy smoker's voice which escaped a toothless disgusting mouth.
"No thanks my friend, we already have what we need" said Walsh in reply, trying to blag his way out of the confrontation.
"Oh ok... no problem" said the tramp. He limped away from them and towards another group and asked the same question with the same results.

They continued walking through the Free zone, trying to hide their disgust as best they could. In the distance the sound of a struggle could be heard and lights from police vehicles shone, disappearing soon after with the sound of a large cheer. As they approached the area, they came across another large crowd who had

blocked a bridge over the river. A police van
which had been pushed on its side was being
looted of riot gear and other objects such as
batons and tazers. A scuffle broke out between
the looters which ended with an unlucky
individual being tasered and flopping to the
ground like a stiff before shaking violently to
the amusemant of some in the crowd.
Anderson was shocked at how quickly people
reverted to their animalistic-like tendencies as
soon as law and order had broken down.
They crept their way through the crowd and
across the bridge, the river still went along with
its quick flow and detritus floated on its surface.

The other side of the bridge was clear of people
and seemed eerily quiet. The police having fled
and the protestors keeping to their side of the
bridge for safety. It was reminiscent of a
medieval siege.
Anderson was looking for any unlocked cars,
walking back to the cottage would take him
days at the least and he didn't feel staying in the
city after dark would be safe.
They were fortunate as many of the deserted
residential roads in the suburbs of their
particular area were filled with abandoned cars
of the older variety. It wasn't long before he
found an unlocked hatchback dating to the
1990s and looking worse for wear, with rusted

bodywork and barely any rubber on the tyres. He smashed the console and changed some of the wiring making it start in a fit of wheezing bangs.

"Wow. They didn't teach us that in basic training" said Walsh.

"Some things you have to learn on your own Walsh. Now get in and study the map, I need directions out of this hell hole" said Anderson, giving the wreck of a car a few revs to keep the engine from conking out.

The roads were deserted, with abandoned cars and burnt out shells of cars interspersed on the roads. Anderson drove quickly but carefully, dodging debris and other objects which had been thrown in the road during the unrest in the nights before. Occasionally groups of people could be seen hiding in street corners or in doorways. Bodies could be seen here and there, those who had succumbed to the illness.

The suburbs gave way to the motorway which was empty as well apart from the occasional police vehicle heading in the opposite direction, people were still following the quarantine rules even after most of them knew anarchy had occurred and they could do what they want. They hoped they would be saved by the government who kept on parroting the line of "Stay calm, help is coming". Those individuals who were intelligent had already left the cities days ago.

It wasn't long before the two men had left the main motorway and were outside the urban sprawl and into the outlying towns which were deserted as much as where they had just come from. They didn't realise that the illness was now taking people rapidly. Walsh turned on the radio, hoping to break the silence which had fallen in the car. There was no reception and the only sound which came out the radio was a monotone white noise.

Their fuel was running low as they entered the vast rural landscape of southern England. They knew they couldn't refuel as the electricity which fed the pumps would be off. They decided they would have to travel as far as possible until the car ran out of fuel and then hike the rest of the way back. It would be gruelling but their military training would help them they knew.

As daylight faded, they entered another suburban blight on the landscape. The road had gone from empty and quiet to that of cluttered and difficult to traverse. Anderson slowed down and zig-zagged his way through the junk which blocked the way. Pallets and other pieces of rubble placed across the lanes of the road and

other wrecks of vehicles which had been abandoned. They finally came to a blockage which couldn't be traversed. Underneath a motorway bridge was blocked with vehicles in all the lanes, the gap between them being too narrow for the small hatchback.
"I guess we're going to have to walk then, according to the map it's only ten miles or so to the cottage so it shouldn't take us long if we walk during the night" said Anderson.
Walsh nodded in agreement as he continued studying the map.

Creeping silently from both sides a group of men made their way towards the car, unbeknownst to Anderson and Walsh. They carried cricket bats and other makeshift weapons and silently crept closer and closer.

Anderson undid his seatbelt and turned off the engine, he opened the door but it slammed back shut and the back window was shattered by a brick. Walsh didn't have time to react as his door was opened and he took a hit to the forehead with an axe-handle which knocked him senseless. Anderson was luckier as he locked his door before turning his sidearm on the man stood in the open door who took a second swing at Walsh who sat slumped in his seat, the axe-handle hit him with a disgusting

crunch and pulverised his windpipe. Andersons'
finger touched the trigger and blew the man's
chest cavity out. He fell back in a mist of blood
and before he hit the ground Anderson swung
round and fired a round out of the smashed rear
window, sending two of the assailants at the
back of the car diving for cover.
Walsh was breathing heavily and making a
terrible snoring noise as he struggled for
breath. Anderson didn't have time to check him
as he clambered out pushing the door open and
emptying another two rounds of lead into the
assailant which was trying to swing a wooden
bat down on his head. The screams which
reverberated under the bridge was haunting but
Anderson didn't hear it through his adrenaline
filled rage, he chased the group away. They
scrambled up the wooded bank of the road and
disappeared through the brush. He fired a few
more shots in their general direction, hoping it
would deter them from returning again.

Inside the car Walsh was fading from life, his
skull fractured and windpipe crushed, his last
few breathes being laboured and loud, his body
clinging to whatever life was left. Anderson did
a medical assessment and knew he couldn't
help in anyway. All he could do was clutch the
dying man's hand and wait until his final flame
of life went out.

Walsh took his last breath and went into that sleep like look of death. Anderson found a blanket in the back of the car and draped it over his comrade as a sign of respect. He wanted to bury his friend but knew it was far too dangerous.

He took one last look at the car before heading Southwards once again on foot. He stopped every few minutes and listened for footsteps or anything else to tell him if he was being stalked by the group of raiders. It was all silent. Only the sound of a fox in the distance calling for its mate and the gentle sound of the wind in the trees above him.

He continued on with determination knowing the ten miles would be a hard trek and dangerous but he would make it. Night fell and cloaked the world in darkness.

<u>Chapter VIII</u>

"Chaos has swept over the world and Civilisation is now collapsing due to it. Fuel, water, food, electricity, gas is all in shortage or cut off completely and most people have no idea what to do. Once the television turns off and they aren't given commands to stay indoors they lose control. The illness is also picking up its pace, the government isn't giving figures now but I imagine it's probably in the hundreds of thousands every day. Across the world it will be in the tens of millions everyday by now."
Rebecca sounded nonchalant as she talked about the collapse of the world around them, making a brew of tea before walking out into the garden with Cyril who carried the other two cups for Robert and Earl.
"So, what do we do after the illness has gone through the population and theirs barely anyone left?" said Cyril.
"We rebuild but that will take time and years. To begin with we will have to survive as best as we can. Find people who will be up to our expectations to join us" said Rebecca.
They sat around chatting in the colourful, sweet smelling garden.
"We should go into the city and see what is happening, maybe it will be empty" said Robert, bored of sitting around.

"We could, but we have to take precautions.
Everyone has to carry something for self-
defence. For all we know the place could be
overrun with looters" said Rebecca.
They all agreed and left soon afterwards,
Rebecca and Robert each carried a Webley
revolver which were over 100 years old and
looked it, while Earl took what he nicknamed
'the shiv', it was a steel pipe sharpened at one
end and wrapped with tape at the other, very
primitive looking but also very deadly. Cyril
decided to take a small wooden bat which could
fit under his jacket snuggly.
Rebecca drove them to the outskirts of the
ancient city and parked in a small wooded area
away from the main road, it wasn't far from
their cottage to the city but they decided to
drive just incase they needed a quick escape if
things got dangerous.
Getting out of the car thy could already tell that
something was wrong, the smell of smoke was
on the wind and getting closer they could see
smoke pouring out of the spire of the cathedral.
The amount of smoke told them that the fire
producing it was of some size.

Walking through one of the many twittens
which were spread throughout the city they
soon reached the centre which was devoid of
people. They could see the inside of the

cathedral flickering due to the fire through the stained-glass windows of which there were many. Cyril could see his old office block in the distance. It was empty and looked even worse than usual with its windows stoved in, he felt a feeling of freedom knowing he didn't have to go there ever again, although life would be hard in the foreseeable future at least he was free.

The silence was broken with the sound of talking down one of the small roads which branched off from the centre of the city. The Group walked towards it and stumbled upon a large mass of people looting a clothes shop, some walking out with clothes piled over their shoulders and in bags which were overfilled. A man walked past carrying a flatscreen television which amused Robert who laughed and asked what the man was going to watch seeing as the electricity had been vacant from the area for over a day now. The man realised that Robert was right and threw the box on the ground before walking into the clothes shop and taking a large bundle of designer clothes which looked far too small for him. The Group stood watching the amusing spectacle for a while before moving on past the ancient city wall which was still standing as it had done since the Roman period of English history.

A huge crash could be heard and they all turned around at once to the sight of the cathedral spire crashing down and through the main body of the building in a roar of noise. The dust cloud which was hundreds of feet high was almost as impressive as the building itself and replaced the area where the spire was only seconds before. A large gust of wind from the collapse blew through the street and made them cover their eyes as the dust followed like some kind of miniature storm with the thousand-year-old stone being turned into flakes.

As they regained their sight after being engulfed by the cloud they emerged and saw a large truck driving from the south road towards them. It had a group of six men in the back and two in the front, all wearing stolen police riot armour and carrying batons. At seeing the vehicle Cyril noticed the looters started to flee extremely quickly down the alleyways and twittens.
The truck pulled up next to the curb and the group in the back lept of the sides, all landing awkwardly due to the armour they were wearing.
"We need to start moving" said Cyril.
"No, no. Let's see what these thugs have to say to us" replied Rebecca.
The group of armoured thugs looked

threatening but ridiculous at the same time. The armour they wore didn't fit them correctly and jostled as they walked. Their headwear was a mixture of Second-World War era replicas, motorcycle helmets and one was even wearing a sieve. The latter man caused Rebecca to laugh.

"Empty your pockets" shouted the man at the head of the group, he was their leader The Group supposed. He wore a police vest which had multiple gold chains draped over his neck and his fingers were covered in rings of all kinds, all of them stolen. In his hand he carried a large machete looking knife which was clearly blunt.
"Come on I haven't got all day, empty your damn pockets" he repeated. Getting more irritated.
"Yeah come on" shouted one of his henchmen, who had an oversized, open-faced motorcycle helmet on his head which bobbled around as he moved.
"I haven't got anything in my pockets and even if I did why should I give you anything, you thuggish brute" said Rebecca.
This comment took the leader of the raider group aback. People usually fled from their presence and nobody had ever answered him back. In his small animalistic reptilian brain, he became enraged. He became red in the face and his only instinct being to swing his blunt

machete at Rebecca who stood ready.

His blade swung back towards Rebeccas head
and she expertly ducked below it before putting
a bullet through the brute's skull dropping him
instantly. His henchmen flung themselves at the
group. Earl fought of two of the assailants with
skill. His shiv brutalising one of them and left
them on the pavement writhing in excruciating
pain as his blood leaked along the ground and
dripping into the drain only a few feet away. The
other assailant fled back to the truck. Robert
fired a few shots at the sieve headed man hitting
him square in the chest and knocking him down
into a dead heap before turning the barrel on
the other thug. He pulled the trigger and the
ancient Webley revolver was silent. The
mechanism clicking, it had jammed. The thug
noticed this and threw himself onto Robert and
a violent mêlée ensued. Robert tried his best to
smash the man's head into the ground and had
the advantage of agility but the man was bigger
than him and threw him off. He carried a sickle
shaped knife and it caught Robert in the arm
and leg, causing him to wince at the cold steel
biting into his flesh.
Rebecca saw what was happening and brought
the muzzle of her own revolver down towards
the thug attacking Robert. Pulling the trigger
and blasting him away, his screams mixed with

those of the other thug bleeding out on the
pavement. Creating a strange opera of agony.
Robert tried to stand but couldn't without
falling back down.

Cyril was trying his best to fight off one of the
thugs with his small bat with great difficulty. His
enemy was larger than him and was proficient
with the iron rod his swung round his head.
Cyril was lucky to jump out of the way of each
swing. His fight or flight response kicked in and
he saw red, like a force had taken over his body.
Rushing towards the thug and knocking him
over before swinging his bat down on the mans
exposed face. He heard the bone crunch as his
nose exploded into a mess of blood, bone and
muscle. His rational mind was gone as the
adrenaline took over and the bat kept swinging
down on the thug's head, beating it into a messy
pulp.

The other three thugs had rushed back to the
truck, screaming expletives at The Group before
telling them they will be back. and speeding off
down he southern street.

"Robert where are you hurt, show me" said
Rebecca, rushing to his aid.

"My leg and arm, it's bleeding." said Robert.
Rebecca tore his shirt revealing a large wound
under his arm which was pumping blood, a
blood vessel had been severed. She made a
makeshift tourniquet and applied it above the

wound, stemming the blood flow somewhat. The leg wound was very much the same, although the cut was much deeper. She applied another makeshift tourniquet on his leg, taking a belt from one of the dead thugs and stemmed the blood flow although not completely. Her hands were covered in crimson and she tried to wipe it off on her dress.

Cyril was out of his trance, looking down at his hands at what he had just done but feeling no guilt or regret. Telling himself it was survival or death.
Rebecca tapped him on the shoulder and knocked him out of his thoughts.
"Cyril...Cyril listen to me" she said, getting his attention.
"Robert is hurt, we need to get back to the car now. Help lift him with Earl."
Cyril nodded, he could hear the seriousness in her voice and immediately helped Earl lift Robert.
They carried Robert with some difficulty trying not to cause him pain as they lumbered back towards the car parked at the edge of the city. Rebecca followed closely behind them just incase the group of thugs decided to make an appearance once again, she didn't have many shots left and had Roberts Webley in her other hand.

Roberts screams of pain caused Cyril anxiety, but he kept on going as his arms felt heavy and tired from the strain.

It took them ten minutes to walk the small distance with no sight of the gang, although their spies were watching proceedings from afar. Robert was put in the back seat of the car, half upright and unable to move, Cyril squeezed in next to him while Rebecca got into the front passenger seat and Earl drove. The speed at which he drove caused Cyril even more anxiety, he was surprised they even survived the journey with the car flying around corners double the speed limit and even getting air at one stage on a small bobble in the road.

They arrived back at the cottage and hastily got Robert inside. Rebecca began trying to work on his wounds, using antiseptic and other medicines to stop the bleeding and anaesthetic to numb his pain. After shoving a needle of some clear liquid into Roberts leg Cyril saw his face physically relax as it numbed the area. Rebecca was working on Robert for what seemed like a lifetime before walking over to the window, her head drooping in sorrow. Cyril walked over to try and find out what was going on and comfort her.
"How is the situation?" said Cyril

"He's not going to make it Cyril, he's lost to much blood. The drugs will only keep him going for a few more minutes so I suggest you say what you have to say to him" she whispered, trying to not be heard by Robert.

Robert was lying on the table, his chest moving up and down in large, difficult breathes. His skin and clothing were covered in dried blood which had turned an extremely dark red, it had also begun to seep into the wood of the table turning it the same colour.

"Robert, its Cyril, you're doing well so hang in there. Once this all over we can have a few pints down the pub again." Cyril was trying to hold back his emotions, although the man dying in front of him had kidnapped him only a few days before he knew there was never any harm going to be done to him now.
"I would enjoy a pint right now" said Robert in a croak and a slight smile on his pale face.

Rebecca was still at the window when Earl ran in from outside.
"Those thugs are back; they are coming up the driveway. Two trucks of them" said Earl.
she slammed her hands down on the worktop in anger.
"Up the Trundle. That's the last place we can

go." she said. Looking down at Robert she began to cry.

"Leave me with the Webley and I will hold them off for a while for you. I'm going to be a gonna soon anyway, I can feel it" said Robert in a fading voice.

Rebecca choked up and had tears running down her face, handing him the Webley which he weakly held towards the door. She hugged him one last time.

"We will meet again one day Robert." she said wiping her tears from her cheek.

"Indeed, we will, now go" he replied.

Cyril and Earl both shook his hand, Roberts skin was becoming colder and colder as he became closer to death. They left with Rebecca out of the back door and through the garden jogging as they could see and hear the trucks turn up at the cottage. Then the shouts of the thugs trying to get in the house. The splintering of wood told them that the house had been breached after its brief siege. And then the sound of the Webley as Robert picked off a few of the bandits before it went silent. The sounds of shots changed to that off shouts and a scuffle.

They didn't stop as they struggled through the thick woodland, their skin and clothing being torn at by brambles and holly. Earl was at the back following Cyril and Rebecca who was at the front, filtering her way through the undergrowth.

Cyril looked back and could see the bandits beginning to enter the woods themselves, getting caught up in the brush due to their cumbersome armour. There were ten that Cyril could count.

It wasn't long before they were making their way up a steep gradient which was the base of the ancient Trundle, it's summit bare and void of trees compared to the thick woodland at the base.

The cottage which stood in between the thicket of trees began to smoke, before flames could be seen licking the wooden interior and the windows glowing orange. Robert in his last act of heroic glory set the house alight by turning on the stove and throwing anything flammable on it. Some thug's could be seen trying to scramble out of the building like rats from a sinking ship, coughing in fits. It was only moments before the flames turned into a torrent and the place was engulfed in a veil of smoke. Many centuries disappearing into smouldering ash to give time to those of the present now making the life and death escape.

The barren landscape of the Trundle could be felt by the group immediately, with the breeze battering their faces with cold air. They all struggled as they moved up the hill, breathing heavily due to the physical strain. Passing through where the ancient gateway would be, they made it to the summit and turned around to make their final stand. They could see their assailants following them, they were just reaching the gateway and looked exhausted. Making the slog up the side of the hill in their armour had taken a toll on their stamina. Some of them heaving for breath as they walked the last part of the summit. They stopped for a moment and faced the three on the summit who stood defiantly above them, their weapons ready.

"Come on then, we've got nothing to lose" said Rebecca, goading the egotistical group of bandits further towards them. It was three against ten, Cyril thought it was a death sentence, they couldn't beat those numbers even though they had a stamina advantage and looked down upon them from the centre of the hill giving them a height advantage.

The thugs moved forward with a crawl carrying their ramshackle blades and blunt instruments. Earl and Cyril readied their weapons and Rebecca aimed her revolver pulling back the hammer but before she had time to pull the trigger the first thug who was only a stone's throw away dropped his club and began clawing

at his neck, his face going red and his eyes
streaming. The other thugs looked at him with
surprise.
"John? What's wrong?" said one of them who
was stood a few feet from him.
The thug dropped to the ground and began
rolling around like he was in flames before
stopping and shaking like he was having some
kind of seizure.

Rebecca saw what happened and looked at Earl
who was just as shocked as she was. Cyril
wondered if the man had just suffered a heart
attack. His thoughts were quickly dashed as
another thug in the group began suffering the
same symptoms and started to struggle at his
own neck like he was being strangled by an
unseen force.
The weather had changed quickly with the day
going from sunny and clear to one of clouds and
storminess, the wind getting more and more
cold and battering.
"What on earth" said Cyril watching as the
entire group of thugs began to start squirming
and struggle to the floor before shaking. One by
one they stopped shaking and became still. Cyril
looked around wondering if they had been
taken out by someone nearby, thinking maybe
Robert had somehow miraculously survived
and helped them but saw nothing. He looked

behind him and for a fraction of a second saw a shadowed silhouette of a figure standing at the bottom of the summit, entirely coloured in the deepest black and with no defining features much like the ones who attacked him during his sleep. He noticed and turned his head back towards the area and it was gone as if it had morphed into the woody surroundings behind it.

"What just happened?" he said to the others as they walked over to the corpses of the thugs to inspect them.
The faces of the corpses were frozen in pain and shock and their throats red from the clawing.
"It looks as if they were strangled or choked somehow but it can't be possible" said Earl.
Rebecca was silent as she studied them more, rolling one of them over onto their back with her foot.
"They died because they had no honour, once they stepped through the gateway into this sacred area, they were at the will of those we can't see" she said.
"You mean the Archons did this?" said Cyril.
"Possibly. It is only my guess, what or who else could have made six men randomly die like this?" she replied pointing towards the group of bodies.

The smoke filled the valley below them as the house continued to smoulder. Looking across the horizon they could see multiple stacks of smoke rising into the atmosphere as the chaos reigned over the world.

From their viewpoint above the landscape they could see for miles upon miles around even in the cloudy gloominess. They could also see the sea and its waves lapping in against the Southern coast. Further out the waves were much choppier and not a single ship could be seen riding the waves.

The group moved away from the corpses and sat down at the peak of the hill looking out for any other bandits who might be looking for them.

"I think I saw a shadow person standing at the edge of the stand of trees" said Cyril

"That's not surprising, they are always observing us and keeping watch, especially in an area such as this. I didn't realise they could take life so quickly though, I only thought they could take life force slowly over time" said Rebecca. She sounded depressed and talked longingly about her escapades with Robert over the years, mostly to Earl but also to Cyril who sat quietly.

Chapter IX

It seemed so peaceful to Anderson walking down the empty country lanes in the evening twilight, with only the sound of his footsteps and nature to accompany him. He walked past empty cars and houses of people he once knew in his childhood but hadn't seen in many years, past shops and pubs he used to frequent now empty of their belongings and like shells of their former selves.

It felt a relief for him to get out of the urban sprawl of the capital and its surrounding tendrils and be back in the wild Sussex heartland with its hedgerows, woods and fields. He knew it was a sad shame that so many of the proud folk of the area would have perished from the illness and with them many parts of their culture, language and history.

The road seemed to wind onwards and onwards as he went deeper and deeper into the countryside. For the ten miles he walked he didn't see one soul. It was almost like everyone had disappeared into nothingness and he was the only person left in the world. There was still a vast array of animals which disported themselves over the empty landscape, taking advantage of the abandonment to investigate former human dwellings, vehicles and other items which they never would have come close too only a month before. Anderson saw on his travel back to the cottage a fox which was rooting around in an abandoned house, making its way out with a loaf of bread in its mouth before fading back into the undergrowth with its spoils.

Walking down the small gravelled track towards the ancient cottage filled him with slight nervousness which was quickly dispelled when he could smell smoke on the breeze. He imagined that it was only the Group who had lit a fire in the fireplace as the days were starting to get colder as they headed into Autumn. He also acutely noticed tyre tracks on the gravel, which were very recent, his Internal Security detective skills rising to the surface. Someone had driven down the driveway recently he surmised and as he got closer, he could see the parked up pick-up trucks which had their doors open, it was just after this that he noticed the charred remains of the cottage, with its roof caved in and the wooden beams all piled in the middle like a ribcage. There was still a huge amount of heat coming from the ashes and he had to stay almost at the edge of the woods to not feel uncomfortable from the heat which radiated outwards. He could see some half-charred remains of men where the doorway

would have once stood. From afar he could see them and didn't recognise their scraps of clothing. He quickly realised the Group had been attacked in some way and their cottage had been destroyed in the struggle.
He looped around the building to the back garden which was very much intact with some frayed flowers which had wilted in the heat of the blaze. The walls were blackened by soot and smoke and he could see the smoke drifting out of the windows and up through the canopies of the trees. Through the backdoor embers were visible still burning in the floorboards and created an orange glow for the internals of the building.

He looked around and found footsteps in the damp soil leading off into the woods and began following them. The protocol for emergencies was to escape to the Trundle so he headed in that direction and followed the footsteps which led him towards it. He noticed that branches and twigs were broken and pushed out of the way as if someone had kept getting snagged in the brush of the thick woodland.

He pushed through the undergrowth still following in the direction of the Trundle and began walking up its steep bank towards the ancient gateway which was built all those

thousands of years before in the Iron Age. The
banks were slippery after a slight drizzle of rain
and he struggled up the side, still looking for
footsteps which he lost in the grass. He could
see the ancient gateway ahead and the slight
ridges beside it which would have once been the
base of a large wooden palisade wall. The wind
was beating him at such a height with the view
of the surrounding landscape being something
to behold, although he had seen it many dozens
of times in his life. Smoke stacks in the distance
showed where all the major settlements in the
area were, the main one being Chichester with
its now empty skyline.

He found more grip walking on the worn-out
muddy path which was formerly used by dog
walkers and day hikers mainly. Going through
the gateway he sensed a change in the air, like a
force was present on the ancient hill. Once he
was over the threshold of the gateway and
palisade, he spotted three dots at the summit of
the saucer shaped hill, they were all sat huddled
and in front of them the remains of a group of
men. As he got closer, he saw the three
individuals stand up, the one at the front
cupped their hands over their eyes to get a
better view before shouting "Anderson!".

He didn't shout in answer but waved instead, he
didn't have enough oxygen in his lungs to shout
after climbing up the side of the hill.

They came to meet as he was still walking towards them, they filtered through the corpses with Rebecca leading them.
When they were within a close distance Rebecca threw her hands around Anderson and gave him a hug.
"It's so good to see you brother, we didn't think you would make it after all that has happened" she said with happiness.
"I am a man of my word and I told you I would be back once the collapse occurred. How are you all doing anyway? and where is Robert?" he replied.
"Robert didn't make it, he perished in the cottage keeping this scum from reaching us" she pointed at the group of corpses with disgust.
"They attacked us in Chichester but we fought them off and escaped. Robert was injured and bleeding out. I tried my best but... but couldn't save him. He told me to go while he held them off." Her eyes began to water again at the thought of her old and loyal friend who perished in the cottage, dying with honour to save his friends.
"He went out how he lived. And his death will not be in vain" Said Anderson.

They began to talk and discussed Andersons' findings while he was undercover in the

Internal Security, he explained how the government had practically kidnapped an entire hospital ward of scientists and teachers. He relayed his experiences on the streets of the capital, the chaos which had occurred and the loss of his friends like Walsh.

Rebecca soon explained to him how everything over the past month had expired, and introduced him to Cyril who he gladly welcomed as a new member of the Group. As they continued to discuss the goings on in the New World which now confronted them time went by and the clouds drifted overhead. They formulated their plan which would mean they had to stay under the radar for a few weeks or even months and survive, hoping some other gang of thugs wouldn't find them and dispatch them which would end their grand plans on how to rebuild the world.

While the siblings conversed on their own Cyril and Earl spoke to each other and looked through the belongings of the fallen thugs. They didn't have much, mostly useless jewellery they have pilfered from unsuspecting innocent people and pockets full of money which they hadn't realised was now completely worthless as there wasn't an economy to support cash.

"I wonder how long people will realise that the most priceless objects for the foreseeable future won't be gems or precious metals but food and water, warmth and shelter. You can't eat banknotes or gold bars" said Earl.

Rebecca and Anderson debated on and it became heated at some points with them screaming at each other with their relevant points but always came to a compromise. They decided that they would stay in the countryside, find a nearby house which was secluded to live in and hoard a months' worth supply of food and water from whatever they could scavenge in the area. After a month they would then spread out farther and see what was going on and then choose their course of action. Cyril and Earl both agreed as it sounded reasonable to them.

They made their way down towards the ruins of the cottage which was still smoking and was now a bed of embers. As the sun set it let off a great heat which warmed the cold which was blowing in from the south.
Rebecca looked over the ruins silently and began to sob once again. Her cottage which had been in her family for generations and her friend which had made his final stand within. It would be a long time before she felt the same as she did before. Cyril saw her sobbing and walked over to her, wrapping his arm around

her for comfort before grabbing her hand and walking with her towards the car.

Rebecca and Cyril got into her old and trusty Sedan while Earl and Anderson took one of the pickup trucks used by the thugs and set off down the road, of which they didn't know where they were heading.

<u>Epilogue</u>

It only took a few weeks for such a technologically advanced world to collapse back into one of the Iron Age, in which the people who were left fought like animals for the smallest of things which people a year before would not have even given a second look.
A loaf of bread in this New World was regarded as a treasure to a population which had once had a constant flow of food. A wasteful population suddenly began to realise that once their civilisation was gone then they couldn't waste anything if they wanted to survive. Those who couldn't adapt did not survive, as nature commands of all of its subjects.

After the initial storm of chaos which swept across the world those who survived settled into a more basic form of existence. And due to the large amount of empty space their was no warfare over land or materials like there had been in the past. People were in some cases sad of losing there past lives in civilisation but also happy now that they no longer had to slave away for a pittance or be told what to do and think.

They never knew how many people truly perished in the collapse but the population of the world was well below the peak it was before. Some of the more mathematically minded of those who survived believed only one percent of people survived the catastrophe. And due to the primordial state afterwards the number would be even lower due to lack of healthcare clean water, a ready supply of food and other services.

In the wider scheme of things nature which had suffered for so long under the oppressive regime of modern society and its constant want of land and materials was suddenly free once again and quickly colonised the former urbanism which had spread like a cancer over the face of the planet. It wasn't long before roots and branches broke apart the brick and mortar and swallowed the concrete in wood and organic matter.

Most people were not prepared for such a catastrophe, a few individuals who had vast supplies of food and water stored away survived for a while before their supplies ran out or was taken from them by groups of hungry scavengers. Those who grew their own food survived even longer, however, the first winter was one of unprecedented hardship. People had never felt cold like it. Rivers and streams froze over in a display not seen for over 200 years in

most parts of the country and across the world
the environment began to settle back into a
normalcy seen before the industrial revolution.
It would be many decades before nature was
fully back to health however.
Some groups dealt much better than others at
the change in civilisation, and some didn't even
notice what had occurred. One of these being
the Sentinelese people who still followed their
hunter gatherer lifestyle and only noticed that
the strange people who flew over them stopped
harassing them. The Amazon tribes who had yet
to be discovered were very much the same and
that great forest they lived within began to claw
back the land taken from it.

And so, the people settled into their new
existence which wasn't very new as it was much
like the lifestyle of their ancestors which lived
many millennia before.

They began to rebuild.

Printed in Great Britain
by Amazon

63644253R00098